When did Pete Kayn

"Sorry, I thought you were gone already."

At the sound of Pete's voice, the voice of her friend, Elissa snatched her gaze away from his chest to find an awkward, embarrassed look on his face. She half turned and gestured vaguely toward her room. "I think I sort of slipped into a coma last night."

"Me, too."

She forced herself to meet his eyes as if nothing out of the ordinary was going on, that she hadn't just ogled the pectorals of one of her best friends. "Are you late for work?"

He shook his head. "On this afternoon."

She glanced at the bathroom behind him.

"Sorry," he said again, this time moving out of the doorway to give her access. "I've got errands to run."

Pete hurried past her toward the guest room. Unable to help herself, she glanced over her shoulder. Damn, his back was every bit as well cut as his chest, a fact she would have been much better off not knowing. Even after he slipped into the room and shut the door behind him, she didn't move. Memories started tumbling through her head, and she realized she'd never seen Pete without a shirt on. And now she feared she'd never be able to forget the sight.

Dear Reader,

What if you found your true love in, literally, the boy next door? The one who'd been your friend for years? That's the stunning possibility facing Elissa Mason when her good friend Pete Kayne loses his home to a tornado and moves into her guest room. One moment he's the good guy deputy sheriff, and the next he's the sexy man she can't stop thinking about. As Pete, Elissa and the rest of Blue Falls pick up the pieces after the tornado, these two friends find a love neither expected.

I love friends-to-lovers stories, so I had a lot of fun writing *Marrying the Cowboy.* I hope you enjoy Pete and Elissa's journey to their happily ever after and the return trip to Blue Falls, Texas.

Trish

MARRYING THE COWBOY

—

TRISH MILBURN

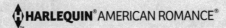

HARLEQUIN® AMERICAN ROMANCE®

Recycling programs
for this product may
not exist in your area.

ISBN-13: 978-0-373-75503-5

MARRYING THE COWBOY

Printed in U.S.A.

HARLEQUIN®
www.Harlequin.com

ABOUT THE AUTHOR

Trish Milburn writes contemporary romance for the Harlequin American Romance line and paranormal romance for the Harlequin Nocturne series. She's a two-time Golden Heart award winner, a fan of walks in the woods and road trips, and a big geek girl, including being a dedicated Whovian and Browncoat. And from her earliest memories, she's been a fan of Westerns, be they historical or contemporary. There's nothing quite like a cowboy hero.

Books by Trish Milburn

HARLEQUIN AMERICAN ROMANCE

To the art department at Harlequin for all the gorgeous covers you've given me. You've made me a very happy author.

And to anyone reading this who's ever had a tornado rip through your life. My heart goes out to you for your loss, and I'm awed by your strength in the aftermath. As I write this dedication, it's only been a few days since the massive tornado devastated Moore, Oklahoma, and more tornadoes hit Shawnee and other parts of Oklahoma. My heart aches for the loss of life, homes and livelihoods.

Chapter One

Ominous. That's the word that came to mind as Elissa Mason stared at the western horizon from the front porch of the house she shared with her aunt. Angry, dark clouds were doing their best to snuff out the last sliver of daylight hanging at the edge of the world. A gust of wind pushed the wisps of hair that had escaped her ponytail into her eye and sent a soda can careening end over end down the street.

Verona, her mother's older sister, came out of the house behind her. "Looks like we might finally get an end to this drought."

"It's what is coming along with the rain that I'm concerned about." Already they were under severe thunderstorm and tornado watches for the remainder of the night. As thunder rumbled in the distance, Elissa couldn't kick the bad feeling she had.

"Yeah, might be a doozy, but beggars can't be choosers," Verona said.

There was no denying that this part of central Texas was in dire need of rain. The ground was so dry throughout the Hill Country that it was cracking, and already ranchers were having to sell off stock because they didn't have adequate grazing. Not to mention the fact that even native Texans were getting tired of baking every time they stepped foot outside, no matter the time of day. It was almost autumn, and there still hadn't been any relief from the heat. The only ones who were likely seeing any benefit from this Hades-like weather were the electric utilities fueling all the air conditioners running nonstop.

As she watched the sky darken, she noticed Pete Kayne turning onto the street in his sheriff's department cruiser. She waved as he pulled into his driveway next door. When he shut off the engine and got out of the car, he glanced back to the west, as well. Another gust of wind had him grabbing his Stetson to keep it from taking flight.

"Looks like you might have a busy night," she said.

He took off his hat and ran his fingers through his dark hair. "That's what I'm afraid of. Going to try to catch a nap in case I end up having to go back in."

She smiled. "Good luck with that." While she was a morning person, Pete Kayne definitely wasn't. Sometimes she gave him extra-bubbly greetings in the mornings when he had to work first shift just to see the annoyed look on his face.

He gave her one of those looks now, the type shared by people who'd been close friends for a long time. She laughed as he headed into his little house. After watching the sky darken more, Elissa headed inside. She checked the weather coverage on TV until it started getting repetitive.

"We better go ahead and eat in case we lose power," Verona said as she headed toward the kitchen.

"Not a bad idea."

As they ate several minutes later, Elissa flipped through some nursery supply catalogs she'd brought home from work.

"Are they still planning to start on the addition Monday?" Verona asked.

A zing of excitement shot through Elissa as she envisioned the pottery studio in its completed form, a place where locals and tourists alike could come and learn to make their own pottery. And the new florist shop she was adding to her already thriving nursery and landscape décor business would boost sales during the parts of the year when people weren't landscaping. "Yeah. I'm having to rein myself in when I look at these catalogs. I could spend myself into bankruptcy with all the neat stuff in here."

Verona smiled. "Like taking a sugar addict into a candy store."

Even with the newly minted loan she'd received for the expansion, Elissa couldn't afford everything she wanted for the nursery. Like her best friends, India and Skyler, she had big dreams for her business, ones that often outpaced what she could bring to fruition.

Verona patted her hand. "You'll get there, honey. Just look at everything you've done in a few short years. Paradise Garden is a destination now, not just a place where locals pick up something to stick in their flower beds."

Elissa was proud of how she'd taken what had once been a little, family-owned nursery she'd worked at as a teen and turned it into a flowery, fragrant, sprawling manifestation of her dreams. That didn't mean she couldn't dream even more. The day she stopped dreaming about what Paradise Garden Nursery could be was the day she needed to hang it up.

After they finished eating and cleaned the dishes, Elissa plopped down on the overstuffed chair to do some realistic choosing of stock she wanted for the pottery studio and florist shop. Verona turned the weather back on and picked up her knitting.

Elissa fell so far into her work that she didn't look up until Verona switched off the lamp next to her chair then clicked off the TV.

"Looks like the storms are tracking north of us, so I'm going to hit the hay. I'm meeting Annabeth for breakfast in the morning."

Annabeth Watson had been Verona's best friend for longer than Elissa had been alive. Along with Franny Stokes and Ingrid Stohler, they played some mad games of poker, too.

"Don't you two get into too much trouble."

"Pffftt," Verona said as she waved off Elissa's teasing warning.

Elissa laughed as she watched her aunt head down the hallway toward her bedroom. A few more minutes of circling products in the catalog and Elissa was yawning. A gust of wind rattled the house as she stood. Hopefully the weather would calm down so she could sleep. Her days started early and were always long, but she loved every minute of them.

Just as she was about to fall asleep, she heard rain begin to patter against her bedroom window. Good. Maybe tomorrow they wouldn't have to water all the plants and shrubs covering the nursery grounds. As she drifted toward sleep, she began to dream she was floating on her back in the middle of a big blue sea.

ELISSA JERKED AWAKE, her heart beating frantically. It took her several of those heartbeats to realize she'd been awakened by the raging storm outside. A loud crash shook the house accompanied by the sound of glass breaking. She leapt from the bed and ran out into the hallway, nearly running into Verona. The tornado siren started howling downtown.

"We've got to get to the storm shelter," Verona said over the wailing of the storm.

A freakish moaning over their heads caused Elissa to look up just as she heard what sounded like an approaching train. Something slammed into the side of the house, and the roof timbers sounded as if they were on the verge of shattering into kindling. The train sound drew closer.

"There's no time!" Elissa opened the hall closet where they kept their jackets and shoved Verona inside. She wedged herself into the cramped space, wrapping herself around her aunt to protect her in case the house disintegrated around them.

The wind howled like a wounded animal intent on retribution. Verona made a sound of distress, half sob and half curse, and Elissa wrapped her arms more tightly around the woman who was like a second mother to her.

"We'll be okay," Elissa said, though she wasn't so sure. It sounded as if the end of the world was upon them.

The angry-beast wailing of the wind mixed with the sounds of crashes and ripping timbers. Elissa feared each moment would be their last, that the house would be swept from its foundation, Verona and her along with it. Her legs began to shake from the strain of crouching on the balls of her feet. The sounds of destruction seemed to go on forever while they hid in the dark, praying the storm didn't find their hiding place.

Gradually, the roar began to quiet. The creaking and popping lessened and then stopped altogether. Even after the storm passed, Elissa didn't move, not fully trusting her ears that it was over.

"We made it," Verona said, spurring Elissa to motion.

Careful not to bonk her head on the coat rod above her, Elissa pressed her hands against the walls of the closet to help her stand. Her legs felt no stronger than boiled noodles. She took a deep breath before she opened the door. Everything was dark, but at least the hallway seemed to still be intact. She reached up to the shelf above the coat rod and fumbled around until she found the large flashlight they kept there.

After helping Verona to her feet, Elissa flicked on the flashlight and pointed it out into the hallway. The family photos still hung on the wall, so at least part of the house was standing. Before investigating further, she grabbed a pair of old sneakers she used when she worked in the yard and slipped them on her bare feet.

Verona followed as Elissa made her way toward the living room. She tried the light switch, but it wasn't a surprise that the power was out. She pointed the flashlight at Verona's feet and saw that she'd slipped on a pair of sandals.

Elissa felt the damp breeze just before she stepped into the living room and found a large tree branch sticking through one of the west-facing windows. Rain had blown in through the broken glass, but that was nothing. They at least appeared to still have a roof over their heads.

"Careful where you step," Elissa said. "The floor is wet, and there's glass everywhere." She stepped over one of the smaller arms of the branch. "I'm going to check outside."

"Be careful. There might be electric lines down."

She looked back at her aunt. "Stay in here."

Verona appeared as if she might argue.

Elissa pointed toward the broken window. "See if you can find a way to close that up around the branch until we can get it removed."

Verona finally nodded.

Elissa wished for daylight as she opened the front door and stepped out onto the porch. The night was so dark that she felt as if she were trying to light her path through a cave with a lightning bug. Thankfully the porch seemed to be intact, though the two rocking chairs were gone. They'd probably been reduced to kindling.

The wail of emergency vehicle sirens started downtown. Hopefully no one was hurt seriously. She pointed the flashlight in that direction and gasped. Pete's patrol car sat upside down in the middle of her yard. She ran down the steps and toward the corner of the house. But when she aimed the flashlight toward Pete's house, it wasn't there.

"Oh, God, no." Heedless of what lay in her way, she ran toward the rubble that was all that remained of Pete's house. "Pete!" A huge lump rose in her throat and panic seized her as she swept the flashlight over the broken timbers and concrete foundation. Pete couldn't be gone. Beyond India and Skyler, Pete was her best friend. Tears pooled in her eyes and her heart ached. "Pete!"

He had to be here somewhere, had to be safe. Why couldn't he have stayed at work?

Loud banging to her left drew her attention. She pointed the flashlight in that direction and spotted the storm shelter halfway between her house and the remains of Pete's. A mangled hunk of white metal lay against the door.

Pete. He had to be the one making that noise. She

made her way through the obstacle course of debris. "Pete? Is that you?"

"Yeah," came the muffled replay. "I can't get out."

Elissa stifled a cry of relief. "Hang on."

She sat the flashlight on the ground so she could shove what had once been his washing machine away from the door. She grunted and cursed when her hands slid off the wet metal. Trying a different tactic, she stooped and gripped the underside of the washer. Gritting her teeth, she managed to roll the useless hunk of metal away from the door.

Needing to see that her friend really was alive, she jerked the door open. Pete climbed the last few steps up out of the shelter. Before she even thought about what she was doing, Elissa wrapped her arms around him and hugged him.

"Hey, what's this?" Pete patted her back awkwardly.

She let him go and took a step away. And then she swatted him on the arm. "You scared me to death."

He glanced past her toward what was left of his home. "You're not the only one." He glanced toward her house. "Are you and Verona okay?"

"Yeah. Tree through the window, but we're lucky." She looked again at the spot where his house had stood for as long as she could remember. "I'm so sorry, Pete."

"It's just a house."

The hitch in his voice told her he wasn't as okay with the loss of his home as he tried to seem. Her heart ached for him. He was such a nice guy, a good friend, and life kept handing him one horrible blow after another. The loss of his father when they were teens, his mother only months ago and now his home and all his possessions. She resisted the urge to hug him again.

He cursed, and when she glanced at him she could tell he'd spotted his patrol car. His personal truck had been in his garage. Lord only knew where it was.

"I've got to get to work, find out how widespread the damage is."

"I'll take you, or you can borrow my car."

"Oh, my God." Verona approached them with another flashlight in hand. "Pete, honey, are you okay?"

"Yeah."

Verona had no reservations about showing Pete how much she cared about him and gathered him into a tight hug. "I'm so glad you're safe." She planted a kiss on Pete's cheek.

Elissa couldn't tell in the dark, but she'd bet money Pete was blushing.

Verona finally let him go and turned to look at the destruction. She shook her head. "It's not fair that we got off so easily while you've lost everything."

"Tornadoes are like that," he said. Pete took a couple of steps then sighed. "I need to go to work. Nothing I can do here now anyway."

"Let me get my keys," Elissa said. She hurried back to the house but paused on the porch to look back toward where Pete stood in the dim glow of Verona's flashlight. Anger welled up in her. Pete didn't deserve this. The guy deserved a break, and already her mind was churning with ways to help him. Because that's what friends did, they helped each other.

PETE FELT NUMB all over, as if he'd been dumped back into a nightmare he'd spent the past few months crawling out of. He didn't think he was a bad guy, but it sure seemed as if fate got a kick out of punching him in the face on a regular basis.

He sighed and shook his head. At least he was alive, and Verona and Elissa escaped unharmed. He only hoped the rest of the area's residents had fared as well. Right now he had to put aside his own problems and focus on work.

"Pete," Elissa called from in front of her house. "Can you help me get the garage door up?"

With the power out, the garage door opener wasn't going to do her any good. He closed the distance and stepped inside the dark interior of the garage. Elissa held a flashlight for him as he opened the door manually.

"You all be careful," Verona said as Elissa and Pete got into Elissa's SUV.

Elissa started the engine and backed out, steering toward the far edge of her driveway to avoid the back end of his upturned patrol car.

"I'll send someone over here to get that out of your yard as soon as I can."

"Don't worry about that now," she said. "It's the least of our concerns."

He deliberately didn't look at what little was left of his home as she drove by. When she stopped at the end of the street, Elissa didn't immediately turn right toward downtown. When he glanced at her, she was staring into the darkness to the left.

"I didn't even think about the nursery until just now," she said. "I need to go check if there's any damage."

"Wait until in the morning. More than likely the power is out there, too."

For a moment, he thought she might actually turn that direction. But after a couple of beats, she turned right and drove him to the sheriff's department. They must have the generator going because lights shone in the windows. Elissa waited until one of the electric co-op's bucket trucks went by before she turned into the parking lot.

"Thanks for the ride," he said as he opened the passenger-side door.

"Be careful if you have to go out, okay?"

He nodded, thankful at least that he had good friends if nothing else.

It wasn't until he walked through the front door that it dawned on him that he was wearing a T-shirt, shorts and the old sneakers he kept in the storm shelter just in case something like tonight happened. His uniforms were probably scattered over half the county. It was doubtful his boots had ended up in the same place, and for all he knew his Stetson was impaled on some bull's horn.

"Been trying to call you." Sheriff Simon Teague gave Pete an odd look, probably because of what he was wearing. Or not wearing.

"Pretty sure my phone flew off with the rest of my house."

"What?" asked Keri, Simon's wife, who'd just hung up the phone.

"My house took a direct hit."

"God, Pete, are you okay?" Keri stood, as if she might check him over head to foot for injuries.

"Yeah. I made it to the storm shelter, barely." He'd almost not been able to pull the door closed, and as soon as he did he'd heard heavy debris hitting the outside as if trying its best to get inside.

"How bad is it?" Simon asked.

"There's nothing left but the foundation and broken

timber." He ran his hand back through his hair, feeling
half-naked without his hat. "And my patrol car is upside
down in Elissa and Verona's front yard."

"Are they okay?"

Pete nodded. "Elissa gave me a ride over here. They've
got a tree in their living room window, but that was the
only thing I could see in the dark." He glanced toward
the 911 dispatch room. Anne Marie Wallace and Sierra
Mitchell were answering calls as fast as they could. "How
bad is everything else?"

Simon's single curse word was enough to let him know
they had a long night ahead of them. Which was good
because he wasn't quite ready to think about all he'd lost
and where the hell he was going to live now.

Chapter Two

It took three tries, but Elissa's call to India finally went through.

"Are you all okay?"

"Yeah," India said. "Ginny is a bit shaken, but she's curled up with Liam now. He's reading her a story to try to get her back to sleep."

"What about Skyler and Logan?"

"They're fine. They just had rain and a little wind out at the ranch. You and Verona?"

"Tree through the window. At least that's all I could see in the dark. But Pete's house is gone."

"Lot of damage?"

"No, I mean it's gone as in completely gone."

India gasped. "Is he okay?"

"Yeah, I just dropped him off at work. His truck is gone, too. And his cruiser is doing a headstand in my front yard."

"I have a feeling this is all going to look so much worse in the morning."

"Yeah. Listen, I'll talk to you tomorrow. The road's a mess, and I need both hands." She didn't tell her friend where she was headed because India would probably spout the same speech Pete had. But the nursery was a huge part of her life. She wasn't about to sleep until she'd seen with her own eyes that it was intact.

"Okay, be careful."

Five minutes later, Elissa wondered about the wisdom of her decision to drive out to the nursery. She dodged downed limbs and drooping power lines. When a gust of wind shook the SUV, she realized she didn't even know if she might be in the crosshairs of another storm. She clicked on the radio and listened to weather and damage reports as she maneuvered through the mess the tornado had left in its wake.

Her heart started hammering well before she reached the nursery, when she came upon the shattered remains of a large cobalt-colored planter in the middle of the road. She tried to drive around the shards, but she'd be lucky if she didn't end up stranded out here with a flat tire.

She crept through the obstacle course of detritus, some of which she recognized and some that had obviously come from nearby homes. Leaves were plastered against strips of pink insulation. A soaked cardboard box was wrapped around what looked like half of a dining room chair.

India was right. This was all going to look ten times worse in the light of day.

The closer she got to the nursery, the more nervous she became. Her heart hammered against her rib cage, and she kept telling herself over and over that everything would be okay. She hit her brakes when she saw the Paradise Garden Nursery sign twisted and hanging by one corner.

"No." She drove the rest of the way and pulled into the parking area, letting her headlights sweep across her life's work.

Tears pooled in her eyes as she saw the front of the building. It looked as if someone had run into it with a bulldozer.

She turned off the car but left the lights on. When she stepped outside, a light rain began to fall. Biting her bottom lip, she walked slowly forward, stepping over broken shards of pottery and twisted metal. The building wasn't completely wiped from the face of the map, but she wasn't going to be open for business any time soon.

She stopped walking and simply stood in the rain, hoping that with each blink of her eyes the scene would change. But it didn't.

The sound of a vehicle approaching was followed by another set of lights joining hers. A car door opened and closed.

"Elissa?"

Even at the familiar sound of Pete's voice, she couldn't pull her gaze away from the building.

Pete stepped up beside her. "You shouldn't be out here now. There's another storm heading this way."

"Tell me I'm not seeing this."

He exhaled. "I'm sorry, Lis." After a few more seconds, Pete wrapped his arm around her shoulders and steered her toward her vehicle. "I really need for you to go home. I can't have you wandering around out here in the dark, exposed. There's nothing you can do now anyway."

His words finally sank in, and she realized he could have just as easily been speaking about himself.

"I'm sorry, Pete. I know this is nothing like losing your home."

He opened her driver's-side door and gripped the top edge. "This isn't nothing." He gave her a sad little smile, knowing just how much this nursery meant to her.

"There's time enough for both of us to face reality in the morning. But right now you need to get home safely and I've got to get back to work."

She nodded. "Be careful."

A growing sense of numbness took hold of Elissa as she made her way back home. None of what had happened tonight seemed real, more like a scene from a disaster movie. The next thing she knew, Godzilla was going to step out of the darkness to stomp on what was left of Blue Falls. But as soon as she drove down her street and saw again the empty spot where Pete's house should be, the horrible reality finally sank in.

She got out of the car to find her aunt waiting for her in the doorway into the house.

"Where have you been? I tried calling, but I couldn't get through."

"The lines are probably overloaded." When Elissa entered the kitchen, she closed the door behind her and leaned against it.

"What is it? Is Pete okay?"

"He's fine." She swallowed past the lump in her throat. "But that's more than I can say for the nursery."

"You went out there?"

"I had to know." She met her aunt's eyes and forced her own not to fill with tears again. "It took a big hit."

Verona stepped forward and pulled Elissa into her arms. "I'm so sorry, honey. But we'll get through this. We're alive. That's all that matters right now."

Elissa knew she was right, that she should be thankful. She was, especially when she thought about how easily Pete could have died tonight, that there still might be people out there who had died or been injured. But that still didn't erase the pain of seeing her nursery in shambles.

Wrung out, Elissa made her way back to bed. But even as tired as she was, she couldn't sleep. Instead, she listened to the patter of the gentle rain and waited for daylight. Even though she knew the light might show her even more damage, at least she'd be able to tackle it. Sitting around waiting and not doing anything was so not her way. It was torture.

She heard a distant rumble of thunder once, but the worst of the weather seemed to have moved on, like a bully who'd thrown a punch and left his victim on the ground holding his bloody nose.

Sirens echoed every now and then through the night, and she wondered what Pete and the rest of the deputies were finding. Once again, Pete was managing to do his job while his personal life fell apart. It made her feel selfish for focusing so much on the nursery, even though she couldn't help how she felt. That place was her livelihood, her life, her dream come true.

And now she faced having to clean up the mess and start all over. Sudden exhaustion pressed down on her, and she closed her eyes and begged for the release of sleep.

PETE FELT LIKE crying when he stepped into the barn at R & J Stables and saw Frankie turn to look at him. But then, it'd been that kind of day. He crossed the distance between them to rub his horse between the ears.

"Hey, boy. Looks like you and I both got lucky, huh?"

Frankie nuzzled against Pete's hand as if he could tell Pete had been having a less-than-stellar day. Pete took a moment to lean his forehead against Frankie's head, grateful that at least he still had this one thing to call his own. And if he'd had to choose which to save, Frankie or his home, he would pick Frankie every time. Named after his grandpa Frankie as a joke, Frankie the horse felt as much a part of his family as his grandpa had, ever since his grandpa had gotten him the horse when he started team roping in high school. Now, the horse was the only family he had left.

"Hey, Pete."

He glanced over as Glory Harris came into the barn, carrying a saddle about half as big as she was. He didn't insult her by offering to help her, though. Glory had been working at her family's stables since she'd been in single digits.

"Not every day I have a sheriff's department cruiser parked outside," she said as she hefted the saddle onto a battered wooden table.

"Only wheels I got at the moment."

"Your truck damaged in the storm?"

"Pretty sure since it blew away along with my house." He tried to make light of it to keep from really dealing with the brutal fact that he was homeless, but a damn lump formed in his throat anyway.

"Oh, hell, I'm sorry."

"Could have been worse." He rubbed his hand along the side of Frankie's neck. "Glad you all were spared."

"Me, too. I don't think I could face losing these animals."

Most of them weren't hers, rather those of boarders, but Glory had never met a horse she didn't fall madly in love with on first sight.

"You going to take him out for a ride?" she asked, nodding at Frankie.

Pete shook his head. "No, too much work to do. I just wanted to make sure he was okay since I was in the area."

She nodded in understanding. "Things settle down, you're more than welcome to come over for a meal or a dozen."

"Thanks." He allowed himself a couple more minutes of the peace he felt with Frankie before he forced himself back to the cruiser and back to dealing with Mother Nature's path of broken lives and dreams.

A couple hours later, Pete's eyes burned from lack of sleep as he pulled into his driveway. Greg Bozeman was hooking his wrecker up to the patrol car to flip it back onto its wheels.

"You look dog tired, man," Greg said as Pete got out of the extra patrol car the department had for when one of the others was in the shop for repairs. Or when one got demolished by a tornado.

"I feel like my eyelids are glued open and I've been body-slammed by the Hulk."

"Yeah, that's about how you look."

Pete flipped Greg the bird, causing his friend to laugh. Considering all the destruction he'd seen in the past several hours, the laugh seemed out of place and welcome at the same time.

"Honey, you look as if you could use some strong coffee." Verona descended her front steps with a coffee cup in one hand and an insulated beverage container in the other.

"You are my new best friend." Pete leaned down and kissed her on the cheek.

"New? I thought I was already your best friend."

Pete smiled. That also felt foreign, but he was thankful for her attempt at levity. He glanced toward the house. "I'm guessing Elissa went out to the nursery."

A sadness passed over Verona's face. "I'm not sure

she slept a wink last night, and she headed out as soon as it started getting light. Only reason I didn't go, too, is that Liam is coming over to get the tree out of the living room and put in a new window."

"I'll drive out there later."

"You need to get some sleep first."

"No time right now."

She gave him a scolding look. "Well, whenever you do decide to get some shut-eye, come back here."

"I don't want to impose."

"Don't be silly. How many times have you cleaned out my gutters or mowed my lawn? I think I can offer you the extra bedroom."

He nodded, too tired to argue.

The patrol car flipped over with the sound of stressed metal and breaking glass.

"I think this one's done for," Greg said with a shake of his head.

Yeah, it more resembled a pancake now than a patrol car. After watching Greg winch the car up onto the flatbed, Pete thanked Verona for the coffee again and headed out for round two.

By the time night rolled around again, he still hadn't found time to drive out to the nursery. Every time he thought about it, something more pressing needed his attention. If he tried to drive anywhere now, he'd more than likely end up in a ditch.

"Come on, man," Simon said as he stopped in front of Pete's desk. "You can crash on our couch."

"Nah, I'm good."

"You sure?"

Pete nodded, though it felt as if that simple action

took the last of his strength. He'd lost count of how many hours he'd been up.

After Simon headed home, leaving Connor Murphy and Jack Fritz on duty, Pete kept sitting at his desk, unable to work up enough energy to move. It wasn't far to Verona's, but it seemed a world away at the moment.

Sierra walked out into the hallway to the drink machine, her headset still on her head. She spoke with someone about a washed-out bridge while she slipped coins into the machine and retrieved some much-needed caffeine. She and Anne Marie had been working every bit as long as the rest of them.

When she ended the call, she walked toward him. "You look like you're about to slip into a coma."

"That's pretty much what I feel like."

"I'm so sorry about your house."

"Yeah, me, too." He rubbed his burning, itching eyes with the heels of his hands then glanced over at Sierra. "Listen, I'm just going to sack out in the back. I'm too dang tired to even walk to the car."

"Okay."

Somehow he found enough energy to push himself to his feet and head back toward the collection of holding cells. Blue Falls wasn't exactly a hotbed of crime, so they didn't have any residents tonight. Pete picked the first stall only because it required the fewest amount of steps to reach and collapsed onto the bunk. It wasn't comfy by any stretch of the imagination, but he was pretty sure he'd sleep like a baby on a concrete floor at this point.

Despite his exhaustion, he stared up at the ceiling and replayed everything that had happened since he'd made a mad dash for the storm shelter he shared with Verona and Elissa, hoping they were already inside. By the time he'd seen that they weren't, it was too late. Going back out into the storm would have been nothing more than suicide.

So he'd sat in the dark listening to the world ripping apart, his heart hammering, praying that they would be okay, cursing that he hadn't had time to get them to the shelter, as well. That was his job, protecting people, and he'd felt like an utter failure as he could only imagine what all the noise above him meant.

Pete rubbed his aching eyes and then forced himself to keep them closed, to try to quiet his mind. But the images kept up their barrage, preventing him from getting the sleep he needed.

The swath of destroyed homes, the uprooted trees, the debris spread across what felt like the entire county. The disbelief and sorrow on Elissa's face as she'd stared at the damaged nursery. Sure, he'd lost his home, but it was just a house, the place where he'd lived after moving out on his own. The things that hurt were those that he couldn't replace, especially the family photos. His heart squeezed, making him wince. He couldn't even take new photos to replace them with his parents both gone.

He shook his head, unwilling to think about that now. His thoughts drifted back to Elissa, to the shocked disbelief on her face that had seemed so out of character. It was rare to see Elissa Mason anything other than smiling or being deliberately ornery in pursuit of laughter. To see her standing there in the rain looking at the ruins of her nursery would have kicked him in the gut even if he hadn't already been reeling from his own loss.

He considered rousting himself and going to her house to make sure she was okay, but his body just wasn't willing to comply. It was as if everything other than his brain had temporarily forgotten how to function. As the thoughts continued to fly, he realized they were making less and less sense. The last thing he remembered before he stopped thinking altogether was the look of relief on Elissa's face when she'd jerked open that shelter door. The edge of his lips ticked up as sleep finally claimed him.

When he opened his eyes again, it felt as if he'd just closed them. He blinked several times, disoriented. It took a moment for him to realize that someone was standing over him, a couple more seconds for the person's face to come into focus.

"Really?" Verona said, her arms crossed. "You prefer a jail bunk to my empty guest room?"

Pete swallowed and blinked a bit more sleep from his eyes. As he lifted himself to a sitting position, he grimaced against the crick in his back. As he stretched the aching muscles, he reminded himself to never do anything that would make him a forced guest in this cell. He was beginning to think the concrete floor actually would have been preferable.

"Well?" Verona said.

"Sorry. I was just too tired to drive over. I did good to make it this far."

"Well, then, I suggest you quit work a little earlier tonight. You give me a time, and I'll have a nice hot meal ready for you."

"Verona, really—"

"Boy, how long have you known me?"

Pete ran his hand over his face. "Forever."

"Then you should know you're not going to win an argument with me." She ruffled his already mussed hair as if he were a little boy.

His heart ached at the gesture, at the memory of his mom doing the same thing. He nodded. "Okay."

"Good. Now if I can just convince that niece of mine to come home at a decent time." Verona turned and headed out of the cell, no doubt shifting her efforts to Elissa.

By the time he put in another long day, he didn't need any convincing to head for Verona's and the promised hot meal. Plus, the lure of a real bed instead of the torture rack of a cell bunk would be enough to make him crawl all the way to his street.

ELISSA STRETCHED HER back and stared at the heaping pile of lost revenue she'd spent the past two days constructing at the edge of the nursery parking lot. Dead plants and shredded lumber mingled with countless chunks of broken pottery and twisted metalwork. The pile was an ugly reminder of all she'd lost in the space of a few minutes, but she couldn't get rid of it until she dealt with the insurance adjuster, whenever that might be.

Like the restoration of electricity, dealing with all the claims in the area was going to take time, no matter how badly she wished she could move both things into the "taken care of" column on her to-do list.

Left with barely any daylight, she turned and dragged her tired, overworked body toward her SUV. Her stomach growled to remind her that she'd not been eating enough to fuel all the work she was doing. Her employees had helped out earlier in the day, but they'd been gone for a couple of hours. She'd worked from near daybreak to dark the past two days, and she still didn't feel as if she'd made a dent.

Still, she couldn't complain too much, not when two lives had been lost at the edge of the county and others besides Pete had lost their homes. At least she had a comfortable place to sleep at night, some peace and normality. Suddenly, nothing sounded better than collapsing into her bed and sleeping for twelve hours straight.

As she drove back into the main part of Blue Falls, the lights blazing in the windows told her that electricity had been restored. When she reached the house and pulled into the garage beside Verona's little car, Elissa didn't immediately get out. Fatigue settled on her along with the realization that if she didn't get more sleep tonight, she was going to run out of steam way before she got the nursery property cleaned up and on the road to recovery. She closed her eyes and leaned her head back, felt herself drifting.

Pecking on the window startled her fully awake. She gasped at the sight of someone standing there, someone not Verona, until she realized it was Pete. With a shake of her head, she unbuckled her seat belt and stepped out.

"What are you trying to do, scare me to death?"

"You've been sitting out here for ten minutes."

"And you know this how?"

Pete crossed his arms and leaned one hip against the fender of her vehicle. "Because Verona and I are hungry, and we were waiting for you to come in."

That's when she caught the distinctive scent of freshly baked bread. Elissa's stomach growled loudly at the mention of food.

Pete smiled. "Looks like we're not the only ones hungry."

"I can't decide if I'm more hungry or exhausted."

"Also know how that feels." Pete nodded toward the door that led into the kitchen. "Come on. She made chicken and dumplings."

Comfort food. That's what they all needed right now, even though dumplings were usually winter fare. She made her way into the kitchen and collapsed onto the nearest chair.

As Verona set a fresh basket of yeast rolls on the table, she squeezed Elissa's shoulder. "You're working too hard, honey."

"It won't get done if I don't work. And the longer it takes, the longer I don't have any income."

Verona slipped into her chair at the opposite end of the table as Pete pulled out a chair between them and sank onto it, looking every bit as tired as Elissa felt.

"All I'm saying is that it won't hurt anything to sleep in a bit tomorrow, both of you."

Throughout dinner, they talked about the storm's aftermath.

"It's so sad about the Claytons," Verona said with a shake of her head. None of them really knew the older couple, but they'd seemed nice enough when they'd come into town from their posts as hosts at the state park campground several miles out of town. They'd been found in the twisted remains of their RV. "But it's a miracle no one else was killed." Verona patted Pete's hand.

Elissa's frazzled emotions had a lump forming in her throat at the idea of how close Pete had come to also being a casualty. She'd never lost a close friend, and the mere thought made her want to cry buckets. And she wasn't even a crier. It was a sure sign that she needed sleep even more than she'd suspected.

"This was delicious," Elissa said. "But I've got to hit the hay before I do a face-plant in my bowl." She started to take her bowl to the sink until Verona waved it back down to the table, indicating she'd take care of the dishes.

"Sounds like a good idea," Pete said, and stood, too.

As Elissa crossed the living area toward the hallway

to the bedrooms, it dawned on her that she had no idea where Pete was staying. She turned to ask him only to find him right behind her. "You're staying here?"

"Yep. Your aunt threatened me with bodily·harm if I didn't."

"I did not," Verona called from the kitchen.

"Close enough." Pete smiled, and even though his fatigue mirrored her own, it was good to see that smile.

She wasn't sure she'd be able to do the same in his situation. It was tough enough in her own.

"You don't mind sharing your space with a smelly boy?"

Elissa actually laughed a little at that, remembering the long-ago comment she'd made when he and Greg Bozeman had tried to sandwich her between them during a particularly sweaty P.E. class.

"As long as you remember to put the toilet seat down, you're safe."

He gave her a salute. "Yes, ma'am."

She rolled her eyes at him and resumed her trek to her bedroom. After making quick work of ditching her dirty clothes and slipping into her pajamas, she snuggled into her comfortable bed. It wasn't until she heard the distinctive squeak in the next room that she remembered the guest bed was just on the other side of the wall, pushed long-ways along the wall as hers was. And for some odd reason, it felt weird to be lying in her bed that close to Pete. When she suddenly wondered what he slept in, she knew she'd gone way, way too long without sleep. She rolled over to place her back toward the wall, but damned if that same question didn't plague her until she finally succumbed to the sandman.

Chapter Three

By the time Pete woke the next morning, the sun was streaming in the window and the little digital clock read 10:30 a.m. And despite the fact that he was in an unfamiliar bed, he didn't think he'd slept that well in months, so much so that he didn't want to move. Since he didn't have to work until the afternoon shift, he lay right where he was for several more minutes, making a mental to-do list. He'd rather go out to the stables for a ride, but he didn't have time. First thing he needed to do was find some cheap transportation. He'd get an insurance settlement eventually, but he couldn't wait that long. He had a mess to clean up next door, and that required a truck.

Though he hated to do so, he forced himself to get up. Nothing on that to-do list was going to get done if he stayed in bed all day. It was likely that Elissa and Verona had been up for hours. But when he stepped into the hall, the house was quiet. Elissa was probably already out at the nursery, and Verona wasn't a woman to sit idly at home when there were things to do and people to help.

He pulled on the clothes he'd taken off the previous night and made his way to the shower. He'd been standing under the hot water for a few minutes when his thoughts drifted to the night before. He'd listened as Elissa moved around in her room, how she seemed to be tossing and turning a lot after she went to bed. He'd gotten the distinct sense that something was bothering her. No doubt it was thoughts of the destruction to her business. Other than that, Elissa had always been carefree and perpetually happy.

As he shampooed his hair, for some reason his thoughts went back much further, to when Elissa had first moved in with Verona at the beginning of their freshman year. He'd been instantly in love. Well, as in love as hormonal teenage boys could get. But he'd also been the world's biggest chicken when it came to girls and had never let her know how he felt, not even when they'd been paired up in history to create a diorama.

They had worked long hours creating the Coliseum in Rome filled with gladiators on the sand and bloodthirsty spectators in the stands, but he still hadn't gotten up the nerve to ask her out. Eventually, the crush had faded away, leaving a close friendship. They'd worked together at the nursery in high school, and she'd been the one to encourage him to apply to the state police academy after his mother's cancer went into remission.

He swallowed hard against the pain that still felt fresh, the knowledge that the cancer had returned and taken her life. He might be a grown man now, but there were times when he still felt like an orphan with both of his parents gone.

Pete shoved the thoughts away as he turned off the water and grabbed a towel. He had enough current problems to worry about without dragging up old sorrows. When he dried off, it hit him that he needed to address one concern before even a new vehicle. Clothes.

He stared at the rumpled jeans and T-shirt he'd had

stowed in his locker at work. Without them he'd still be running around in the shorts and tee he'd had on when the storm hit. He had some new uniforms ordered, but he needed nonduty clothes pronto. Hell, he needed everything. Which meant he had to first go to the bank and get a new debit card. Damn, life was a pain in the ass when everything you owned blew away.

He rummaged in the cabinets until he found an unopened toothbrush. He needed to shave, too, but he'd wait until he could buy his own razor. It was bad enough that he was pilfering a toothbrush. Something about that act caused the events of the past couple of days to slam into him as he finished brushing his teeth. He cursed and shook his head. After rinsing the brush and his mouth, he stood with his hands pressed against the countertop for several seconds as he allowed himself a mini pity party. But then he turned on the faucet, splashed his face with cold water and toweled it away.

Feeling sorry for himself had never worked to his favor, so he wasn't about to start now. Instead, he pulled on his worn jeans, thankful at least that there was one more clean T-shirt in the guest room.

He opened the bathroom door and was greeted with a yelp.

ELISSA COULDN'T BELIEVE she'd slept so late. After she'd finally gone to sleep the night before, she didn't remember anything. Usually she woke up at least once in the night, but not last night. She'd slept like not just a log but a petrified log. She rubbed her hand over her face, trying to wipe away the groggy feeling.

As she reached for the bathroom door, it opened. She came fully awake with a cry of surprise. Her heart hammered against her breastbone until she realized it was only Pete and not some burglar who'd had to take a tinkle break before robbing her blind.

But as she looked up at him and noticed he wasn't wearing a shirt, her heart refused to slow its frantic pace. The bare skin was damp and probably warm from the shower. And when did Pete Kayne get so ripped?

"Sorry, I thought you were gone already."

At the sound of Pete's voice, the voice of her *friend,* she snatched her gaze away from his chest to find an awkward, embarrassed look on his face. She half turned and gestured vaguely toward her room. "I think I sort of slipped into a coma last night."

"Me, too."

She forced herself to meet his eyes as if nothing out of the ordinary was going on, that she hadn't just ogled the pectorals of one of her best friends. "Are you late for work?"

He shook his head. "On this afternoon."

She glanced at the bathroom behind him.

"Sorry," he said again, this time moving out of the doorway to give her access. "I've got errands to run."

Pete hurried past her toward the guest room. Unable to help herself, she glanced over her shoulder. Damn, his back was every bit as well cut as his chest, a fact that she would have been much better off not knowing. Even after he slipped into the room and shut the door behind him, she didn't move. Memories started tumbling through her head, and she realized she'd never seen Pete without a shirt on. And now she feared she'd never be able to forget the sight.

With a shake of her head, she entered the bathroom and locked the door behind her. It wasn't as if she thought

Pete was going to suddenly burst in, but she had the strangest feeling that she needed that extra barrier.

She pressed her hand against her forehead to see if she was feverish. Warm, yes, but she had the awful sense that the warmth had nothing to do with sickness and everything to do with embarrassment.

Even when she shucked her pajamas and stepped into the shower, she couldn't stop thinking about how Pete's lean muscles and toned skin had beckoned to her, begging her to run her hands up and over them. And then her traitorous brain shifted to thoughts of how Pete had stood in this shower naked only a short time before. Her entire body heated up more than could be accounted for by the stream of hot water.

Good grief, either she was having the strangest dream ever or she seriously didn't get enough rest last night despite the fact that she'd been asleep twice as long as usual.

She hurried through her shower, but by the time she'd finished in the bathroom Pete was gone. Even with the house empty, she closed her bedroom door once she stepped inside. She sank onto the side of her bed. Her strange reaction to Pete had to be because of the stress she was under. All she needed was to work, get the nursery up and running again, return life to normal. Her being off-kilter, that's all her weird reaction to Pete was. Nothing more.

With a shake of her head, she dressed and headed to work. When she arrived, she discovered India and Skyler walking back to India's car.

"What are you guys doing here?" Elissa asked as she pulled up beside them.

"We came to see if we could help," India said.

Not so long ago, India wouldn't have been able to be

away from her boutique during the middle of the day. But since getting married and becoming a stepmom, she'd hired some help to give her more flexibility with her time.

Elissa eyed Skyler as she got out of the SUV. "Not really the type of work you need to be doing."

Skyler crossed her arms above her gently rounding belly. "I'm pregnant, not an invalid."

"Okay, okay. Grouch."

India laughed a little, earning a glare from their hormonal friend. "What? She's right. You are grumpy."

Skyler pointed toward India's stomach. "Just wait until you get pregnant."

India didn't say anything in response, but the way her mouth twitched at the edges gave her away.

"Oh, my God," Elissa said. "You already are, aren't you?"

The twitching turned into a smile as India nodded.

Elissa and Skyler squealed at the same time and wrapped India in a group hug.

"Wait," Skyler said as she took a step back. "You knew and didn't tell us?"

"I just found out yesterday."

Elissa swung a pointed finger between her two friends. "That's it. No heavy lifting, no stooping, none of that for either of you."

"Well, how are we supposed to help?" India asked.

"Name your babies after me?"

"What if we have boys?" Skyler asked.

Elissa smiled. "Mason's a nice name."

Skyler rolled her eyes.

Elissa laughed. "Those cowboys of yours don't waste time, do they?"

"Bound to happen when we stay in bed half the time," India said.

All three of them snorted with laughter. It felt good to laugh, to have good news. It felt normal, and that was exactly what Elissa had told herself she needed to get past her temporary lack of sanity earlier.

"It's your turn, you know."

It took Elissa a moment to realize that Skyler was talking to her. "What, to have a baby? Uh, no."

"There's nothing wrong with babies," India said.

"Not when they're someone else's little booger and poop factories."

India shook her head as if saying Elissa was silly to protest. "You would love a baby if you had one."

The image of Pete's bare chest and arms came to mind, along with the crazy thought that she at least wouldn't mind the process of making said baby.

Good Lord, she had somehow misplaced her last brain cell. Maybe it had blown away in the storm and was floating in some Louisiana bayou.

"Is something wrong?" India asked.

Elissa shook her head, perhaps too vigorously judging by the curious looks her friends were giving her. "No, not if you two keep your matchmaking endeavors pointed toward someone else."

"It's not us you have to worry about," India said. "You seem to forget who you live with."

"No, I'm well aware I share a house with the Cupid of Blue Falls. But I've become adept at avoiding her arrows."

Lord help her if Verona were ever privy to how Elissa had responded to the sight of Pete's half-naked body. Heat whooshed through her at the mere thought of Pete's name and the word *naked* in the same sentence.

"Are you sure you're okay?" India asked.

"Yeah, just got to get to work. I'm late getting started as it is."

"Tell us what to do." India turned as if she would follow Elissa inside.

Though their trio spent a tremendous amount of time together, today Elissa just wanted them to leave. Until she purged herself of inappropriate thoughts about their mutual friend, it was too dangerous to be around them. They knew her just a touch too well.

"Really, there's nothing suitable for two pregnant women to do. You really want to help me, go suggest someone to Verona to focus her matchmaking hoodoo on. That's the last thing I need right now."

"Fine, but you're coming with us to the music hall tonight," India said. "There's a band from Dallas playing that Liam says is really good."

"I don't have time." She gestured toward the damaged building as well as the two demolished greenhouses out back. "As you can see, I have a lot of work to do. And the insurance adjuster is supposed to be here today, though I don't know when."

"You've been going almost nonstop since the storm," Skyler said. "You need some downtime."

Elissa started to protest again, but Skyler held up her index finger to indicate she wasn't finished.

"Plus, it's common knowledge that you don't refuse pregnant women. We get whatever we want."

Elissa raised an eyebrow. "Does Logan know this?"

"Intimately," Skyler said with a wicked grin.

Damn if that image of Pete didn't pop into her head again. Her friends were right. She needed to get out, have a night of fun, dance and purge her head of troubling thoughts. Be the person she always was, the life of the party.

But by the time she finished work for the day and dragged herself home, she wondered about the wisdom of agreeing to meet her friends at the Blue Falls Music Hall. After all, there would be time for dancing and flirting after she got the nursery back up and running.

"Hey, honey," Verona said as Elissa stepped into the house. "Dinner will be ready in about twenty minutes if you want to shower and get ready."

Elissa gave her aunt a questioning look.

"The girls told me you all were going dancing tonight."

"I'm too tired."

"I know you're tired, but it'll be good for you to go out. Pete's already finished with the bathroom, so it's all yours."

"Pete?"

Verona smiled. "Yeah, he's going, too."

Elissa's lips pressed together as she took a calming breath. "Don't."

"Don't what?"

Elissa didn't buy the innocent look Verona shot her. "You know what." She glanced toward the hallway to make sure Pete was out of earshot before returning her gaze to her aunt. "Pete and I are friends."

"Which is why it's perfect. You already know you like each other."

"As friends. Jeez, that would be like dating my brother." Well, not exactly. If she had a brother, she was pretty sure she wouldn't dwell on the contours of his chest and abs.

"Just give it some thought."

"No," Elissa hissed as she heard Pete coming up the hall toward them. "Not one word."

Verona sighed and went back to stirring the spaghetti sauce on the stove.

Elissa turned to head to her room, where she was seriously considering locking herself, but she ceased moving when she spotted Pete. He'd obviously gone shopping because his old, worn clothes were gone, replaced by a new pair of jeans, boots and a chocolate-brown shirt. He held a new tan Stetson in his right hand. She'd seen him in similar outfits hundreds of times, but the increase in her heart rate made her feel as if she were looking at him for the first time. Her friend had grown ridiculously handsome without her noticing. And it felt really weird to even think that.

She forced herself to act normally, which was way harder than it ought to be. "Hit the ShopMart?"

"Yeah. Not likely I'm going to find my old clothes."

"You probably wouldn't want them anymore if you did."

"True."

When Elissa met Pete's eyes, she had the distinct impression he, too, was remembering their awkward run-in at the bathroom door that morning. She hated how her easy camaraderie with Pete felt as if it was slipping away, but she was determined to get it back and put this odd bobble out of her mind.

"Well, if I'm going dancing, I better clean up. I'm wearing about an inch of dirt. Doubt I'll get many dance partners like that."

As she moved past Pete, she pictured herself dancing with him. She mentally cursed. She'd danced with Pete a zillion times, and it had never been anything other than two friends goofing off and having a good time. As she stepped into the bathroom, she wondered how in the world she was going to avoid dancing with him until the image of his naked torso didn't taunt her every time she looked at him.

AN HOUR LATER, Pete followed Elissa into the music hall. Even for her, she was walking faster than normal, as if she wanted to get away from him. He couldn't help wondering if it had anything to do with him startling her that morning. But that shouldn't have bothered her. It wasn't as if he'd strolled out into the hall buck-naked.

But something was definitely up because as soon as they stepped inside she scanned the crowd and headed straight for India and Skyler. Fellow deputy Connor Murphy had to do a quick sidestep with his beer to keep from getting mowed down by her.

"What's up with Elissa tonight?" Connor asked as he approached Pete. "She's moving like she's on her way to a fire."

Pete shrugged. "Who knows? Pressing girl talk, I guess."

Connor shook his head. "Women."

Exactly. Just when you thought you had one figured out, she up and started acting strange.

"You been cleaning up your place yet?"

"Haven't had time. Got to get a truck first, but haven't gotten around to that, either. Had to go buy a new life today. It's bad when you've got one pair of underwear to your name."

"Ask Greg. He probably knows someone who has a truck for sale."

Pete nodded. "Good idea." In fact, he saw Greg over by the bar, not too far from where Elissa stood. "I need a drink."

"Later."

Pete made his way around the edge of the dance floor, crowded as usual with locals and tourists. His gaze connected with that of a pretty blonde who smiled at him. He gave her a small smile back but continued on his way to the bar instead of asking her to dance.

"Hey, Pete," India called to him over the sound of the crowd and the band.

He waved, but she motioned for him to come over. As he drew closer, Elissa slipped onto the stool behind her. There it was again, the subtle moving away from him. Or maybe he was imagining it. But why would he be? Shaking off the questions, he directed his attention at India.

"Liam's organizing another rodeo to benefit the tornado victims. Do you think you could get us a list of those affected?"

"Sure."

"And include yourself, okay?" Skyler said.

"I'm fine. I've got insurance."

Elissa shifted forward on the stool. "You know better than to argue with Skyler, even before she was pregnant and grumpy."

"Someday when you get pregnant, I hope you have triplets. And that they're hell on wheels."

Elissa shot Skyler a look of horror. "Bite your tongue, woman."

India laughed, and Pete found himself smiling at the familiar banter between Elissa and Skyler. Whatever weirdness had taken up residence in Elissa seemed to have disappeared, thank goodness. It was bad enough he was forced to invade her home, but he didn't want to make her uncomfortable while he was at it.

Someone touched his arm. When he turned, the pretty blonde stood there.

"Would you like to dance?"

The crazy urge to look at Elissa gripped him, but he resisted. Trying not to read anything into his reaction, he instead smiled and offered his arm to the blonde. "Lead the way."

As his dance partner told him her name was Candace and she was in town for a wedding the next day, he tried to pay attention. He was beginning to wonder if he'd been knocked on the head during the tornado because it was hard to pay attention to her. But he made the effort, even pulling her a little closer.

Before he even thought about what he was doing, he turned his gaze toward where Elissa had been sitting, fully expecting she'd found her own dance partner. Instead, she still sat on the stool, staring right at him.

Chapter Four

Elissa jerked her gaze away the moment Pete looked in her direction. What was up with her? She was beginning to think she'd taken leave of her senses.

"Are you okay?" Skyler asked.

Elissa shoved away her sudden, brain-addled interest in Pete and slipped off the stool. "No. I didn't come here to sit on my butt. This place is for dancing."

"Then go dance."

Elissa made a vague gesture around the room. "Slim pickings tonight. You won't mind if I steal your man, will you?"

Before Skyler could answer, Elissa grabbed Logan's hand and dragged him toward the dance floor. He laughed in her wake.

As they found a spot on the dance floor just as an upbeat tune started, Logan twirled her into the crowd. "One of these days, if you're not careful, Skyler is going to sock you one."

"I'm quicker than her on a normal day, and she's only going to get bigger."

Logan winced. "Be glad she didn't hear that."

"Already touchy about her figure?"

"You have no idea. We had a Chernobyl-style melt-down this morning when she couldn't fasten her pants."

Elissa glanced through the crowd toward Skyler. "Maybe I should lay off for a while, though that's a little like asking everyone in the world to stop posting their cat pictures online."

Still, maybe Skyler and India both could use a little pampering. If she got a bit further along in her cleanup and rebuild of the nursery, maybe she'd suggest a spa day for the three of them. She could even get into shopping for baby things. Being a mom might not be on her radar, but by golly she was going to be the best honorary auntie the world had ever seen. She was going to spoil those kids so rotten their mothers would never forgive her. She smiled at that thought.

"That smile is never good."

Elissa looked up at Logan. "What, this?" She pointed toward her mouth. "I'm as innocent as innocent can be."

"Yeah, right."

Elissa laughed and for a few minutes let go of all the things she could be worrying about if she let herself. She wasn't a natural worrywart as her friends could be, so the past few days had been exhausting both physically and mentally. She had to find a way to deal with restoring her business without letting it fritz her brain and turn her into someone she wasn't.

At the end of the song, a very determined-looking Skyler reclaimed the love of her life.

"Thanks for letting me borrow him," Elissa called after her, then laughed.

In the next moment, Greg Bozeman pulled her into his arms and began guiding her around the dance floor.

"So, when are you and I going to run off and get married?" Greg asked, a big grin on his face.

Elissa smiled back. "As soon as I can stop seeing you mooning the town from the top of the water tower."

"Lord, I'm never going to live that down."

"You are a town legend." Elissa laughed at the memory from their senior year when after a big win that sent the Blue Falls High football team to the playoffs, Greg and a few other players had convinced someone in Austin to buy them a keg of beer. They'd been relatively fine out on the back of Taylor Binghamton's family's ranch. But then Greg had gotten the big idea to moon Blue Falls under the light of a full moon. The only reason he hadn't been arrested was that the sheriff hadn't been 100 percent sure of his identity and Greg had hightailed it. By the time the sheriff had found him the next day, Greg was sober. Still, everyone knew it had been him. And despite his protest now, Elissa was pretty sure he liked being the star of that particular story.

"I guess I'll have to settle for being a swinging bachelor for a while longer."

"Yes, I'm sure it will be a hardship."

Over the course of the next three songs, Elissa found herself dancing with three more partners, two friends and one insurance adjuster from Austin in town meeting with policyholders who'd suffered losses from the tornado. Despite his bore-her-to-death job, he was a fun guy. But as soon as their dance ended and she turned to find herself face-to-face with Pete, she totally forgot Insurance Boy's name.

Pete pulled her into the next song, and she had to fight the totally stupid urge to plant her feet. She had no idea what was going on in her noggin, but if she refused to dance with Pete, she might as well skywrite that she was having odd feelings toward one of her best friends. They'd danced countless times before, just as she always ended up dancing with Greg and a lot of the other regulars at the music hall. Why it suddenly felt different didn't make one lick of sense. But it did. He felt too close, and she was aware of every point at which their hands touched and where Pete's other hand rested at her waist.

She had gone completely loony.

"Something wrong?"

She met Pete's eyes and saw genuine concern there. It touched her more than it should. Pete was just a nice guy, one who cared about everyone.

"Yeah." She shrugged. "I'm more tired than I thought." She stopped dancing and gradually extricated herself, trying not to be obvious about it. "Honestly, I think I just hit the wall."

Pete nodded toward the door. "I don't have a lot of pep tonight, either. What do you say we cut out?"

What she really wanted was some time alone to get her head screwed on right, but she couldn't say that. She had to ride out the rest of this odd trip on the crazy train until life, and her feelings toward Pete, got back to normal.

"Sure."

"You're calling it a night already?" India asked when Elissa told them she was leaving.

"Wow, outdone by the pregnant ladies," Skyler said.

"Some of us have to rebuild our lives," Elissa snapped. "Literally."

Elissa caught the wide-eyed surprise on Skyler's face and immediately felt like a bitch. "I'm sorry."

Skyler grabbed her hand. "No, I'm sorry. I shouldn't

be so hard on you, not now anyway." She pulled Elissa to her for a hug. "Go get some rest."

All the way back to her house, Elissa couldn't stop thinking about how edgy and out of character she'd been acting over the past few days. It had to be stress. Nothing else could explain her mood and actions, the hyper-awareness she was suffering around Pete.

Maybe she'd simply lived too long without a guy in the house. She hadn't lived with her parents for more than a couple weeks at a time since she'd left them to their globe-trotting professions and moved in with Verona at the beginning of her freshman year of high school. So it had been only her and her aunt living in a testosterone-free zone for more than a decade.

"You know we're back, right?"

She glanced at Pete in the passenger seat. "Huh?"

He pointed out the windshield at the interior of the garage. "You planning on falling asleep in your car again?"

She mentally shook herself and reached for the door handle. "I swear, I feel as if I've been losing my mind the past couple of days."

"You're not alone."

Elissa shot a look at Pete, trying to figure out if there was more meaning in his words than what there appeared on the surface, but he was already getting out of the car. Loony. She was completely and utterly loony.

Pete reached the door into the house first and held it open for her. Verona had evidently already gone to bed, because the house was quiet, and only a single lamp was burning in the living room.

"You know what I think will make you feel better?"

Her nerves doing an ill-advised dance, Elissa tried her best to appear normal. "Winning the lottery?"

"Something even better." He moved into the kitchen and retrieved a lemon meringue pie and two forks.

Elissa glanced toward the hallway before returning her attention to Pete. "Put that back. She made it to take to her poker game tomorrow. She'll kill us if we touch it."

Pete gave her a devilish grin she didn't see very often. "When was the last time we got into trouble?"

She thought about it a moment. "Probably when we filled the entire front yard with Oklahoma Sooners decorations." Elissa would dare anyone to find a bigger Texas Longhorns fan than her aunt, and the mere mention of the Sooners was enough to make her growl. Having her entire yard "defiled" had made Elissa worry for the one and only time that her aunt might kick her out of the house.

"So what's a little pie filching compared to the Great Sooner Attack?"

Elissa shook her head. "I'm going to tell her that you ate every bite."

Pete walked past her, tipping the front of his hat up as he headed for the front door. "Then maybe I will."

"Oh, no, you don't," she said as she followed him onto the porch. "You can't tease me with pie and then not share."

He offered her a fork. "Partners in crime?"

She huffed and grabbed the fork.

Pete sat at the edge of the porch at the top of the front steps, and Elissa plopped down beside him. Even with the electricity back on, she could still see the vast array of stars when she looked up at the sky.

"Pretty night," Pete said as if he were reading her mind. "Hard to believe we all about blew away a few nights ago." He glanced to the left, toward where his house used to stand.

"Are you going to rebuild?"

"Honestly, I haven't had much time to think about it." He stuck his fork in the pie then took the first bite.

Elissa cut a bite for herself and *mmm*ed at the tart taste. Verona Charles never met a type of pie she couldn't master.

"I've got to find somewhere to live, though," Pete said as he cut another bite of pie. "Or your aunt is going to make me fat. Every time I step in the house, she tries to feed me. I think she believes I can't feed myself."

"Sometimes I think she wishes she had a family of her own. She would have been a good mom and wife. Maybe that's why she's always trying to take care of everyone in town."

"Don't get me wrong. I appreciate it, everything both of you have done for me."

"We haven't done anything. It's not like anyone was using your room anyway."

"I don't mean just after the storm." He took another bite and took his time swallowing it. "All the time Mom was sick, Verona was bringing over casseroles and cakes. And don't think I don't know you're the one who set up the mowing and gardening brigade."

"I don't know what you're talking about."

He bumped her shoulder with his. "Deny it all you want, but you'll never know how much it helped Mom to see her garden doing so well last spring."

A lump formed in Elissa's throat at the memory, at how the garden had bloomed with more life each day as Pete's mom's had slipped away. Elissa didn't spend that much time with her own mother anymore, but her heart still squeezed with a horrible pain at the idea of losing her. And Pete had lost not one but both parents before he should have. At the thought of how alone he was, how much more alone he'd be without friends, she found herself reaching over and squeezing his hand.

A sizzle of new awareness raced up her arm, but she didn't allow herself to show it. What Pete needed now was a friend, and that's exactly what she was and would always be to him.

Pete gave her hand a brief squeeze back then held the pie up toward her. She realized they'd eaten half of it already.

"If we both wake up with stomachaches, it will serve us right," she said.

"You want to stop?"

"Are you kidding?" She grabbed the pie and took a big bite.

Pete laughed. "Yeah, I guess we need to get rid of the evidence."

"Exactly. And then plead ignorance in the morning."

"Or make sure we're gone before Verona notices."

Elissa stopped with a bite halfway to her mouth, then met Pete's gaze. They gave each other a knowing look.

"Yeah, you're right. Plead ignorance."

They slipped into silence as they devoured the rest of the pie. When Elissa sat with the empty pie pan in her hand, she moaned.

"Ugh, I can't believe we ate that entire pie."

Pete leaned his elbows back against the porch. "Felt good, though, didn't it?"

"For now. Not sure how I'll feel in a few minutes."

Elissa looked up at the sky again in time to see a shooting star. She didn't point it out to Pete. Instead, she used her wish for him, that all the bad things were finally over for him. To her way of thinking, he'd already gotten his life's quota of bad taken care of and was due a great future.

The sound of a truck engine and the rattle of a trailer drifted up the street from Main.

Elissa jerked her gaze to Pete. "God, I just realized I haven't asked you about Frankie. Is he okay? The stables?"

"All safe."

She heard the relief in his voice. At least he hadn't been dealt that blow, as well. That was too horrible to think about. He'd had Frankie almost as long as she'd known Pete. Even though Pete didn't use Frankie to rodeo anymore, he still went riding whenever he got the chance.

"Thank goodness."

"That reminds me," he said. "I hate to ask another favor, but do you have time to run me out to Walter Stone's place in the morning?"

It was on the tip of her tongue to refuse, pointing out that she still had an incredible amount of work to do at the nursery. But she shoved that thought away. Hadn't she just been thinking that Pete deserved to have things go his way?

"Sure. Why?"

"Greg said that Walter has a truck for sale that I can probably afford."

You won't have to drive him places if he gets his own truck. The little voice in her head taunted her, knowing that something weird was going on with Elissa's feelings toward Pete, that part of her wanted to keep distance between them. She mentally smacked the owner of the voice. The odd feelings would go away if she just ignored them. Wasn't the fact that they were sitting out here eating pie like the good friends they always had been proof of that?

After a couple more minutes of enjoying the quiet of the evening, Elissa lifted the empty pie tin. "What am I going to do with this?"

"I have an idea." Pete took the tin from her and stood. When he headed inside, Elissa followed him.

He went straight to the kitchen, grabbing a sheet of the smiley-face notepaper off the pad hanging on the front of the fridge. She watched as he first washed and dried the tin plate then placed it on the countertop. He grabbed a pen and started writing on the notepaper.

"What are you writing?"

He didn't answer, but when he finished he tapped the paper and moved away toward the hallway.

Curious, she checked out what he'd written.

Elissa ate your pie. I tried to stop her, but she was determined.

"Why, you…" Elissa crumpled the note in her hand, turned and ran for Pete.

With a wide smile, he ran down the hallway and into the guest room. She wasn't fast enough to catch him before he closed and locked the door. "You're a rat."

Verona's door opened. "What the devil are you two doing?"

Elissa heard the sound of Pete's muffled laughter on the other side of the door. Keeping the crumpled note hidden in her hand, she said, "Pete ate the entire pie you made for the poker game. I tried to stop him, but he seemed mighty determined to eat the whole thing."

The laughter ceased on the other side of the door. Elissa had a difficult time hiding her smile as she started for her room.

"I hope you know you're going to buy me a new pie in the morning, young man," Verona said as Elissa bit her lip to keep from laughing.

Pete opened his door just as Elissa slipped into her room. The last thing she heard before closing her door was Pete's "Yes, ma'am."

With the door closed behind her, she leaned against it and let the smile form. She felt better than she had since before the storm.

ARMED WITH A new-to-him pickup truck and a day off from work, Pete pulled into his driveway ready to clean up the mess the storm had left behind. But when he cut the engine, he didn't get out immediately. Instead, he sat staring out the windshield, trying not to be overwhelmed. Part of him just wanted to drive away and not look back, but that wasn't going to solve his problems. He needed a new place to live, and while he decided where that would be he might as well dispose of what Mother Nature had left of his previous home.

But first things first. He reached over and grabbed the pies he'd just bought at the Mehlerhaus Bakery. If there was one person in town who was a better baker than Verona, it was Keri Mehler Teague. The woman was a magician with everything from cakes to cookies to bread. She'd been teased on more than one occasion that she added a little something extra into her confections to cause all of Blue Falls to become addicted to them.

He slipped out of the truck and headed across the yard to Verona's. He went in through the open garage and knocked on the kitchen door before stepping inside.

Verona looked up from where she was pouring herself a cup of coffee. "I see you didn't forget your promise."

"No, ma'am." He held up the boxes. "And I brought a little extra insurance so you wouldn't kick me to the curb."

Verona crossed to him to see that he'd not only replaced her lemon pie but added a strawberry one, as well. "I guess this will do."

He saw the smile tugging at the edge of her lips and couldn't help his own smile.

Verona took the pies and placed them on the kitchen counter. "I was just teasing you. I know it was probably Elissa who instigated the pie-napping."

Pete leaned one hip against the counter. "No, actually it really was me."

Verona raised an eyebrow at that. "Well, I'd lay money down that you didn't eat the entire thing yourself."

"No, I had a little help."

"Good. That seems like her, and she's not been herself lately."

"No surprise why. That nursery means everything to her. She's holding up pretty well considering." She seemed tired and distracted, but how could she be anything less?

Verona shook her head. "No, something else is up with her. Maybe you could take her out for dinner tonight, try to figure out what it is."

Speaking of odd, something was off about Verona's request, but he couldn't quite put his finger on it. "Why don't you ask her?"

Verona gave a little snort. "Hon, I helped raise that girl. She's as likely to tell me if something is bothering her as she would her mother."

"What makes you think she'll tell me?"

"Well, you're already stealing pies together. I figure that points to a certain level of trust."

Pete shook his head. "I'll ask if the topic comes up, but you know Elissa. Most things just roll off her back. And if they don't, she's not inclined to spill the beans about it."

Verona patted him on the arm. "Just try. She's always considered you a very good friend, and sometimes it's easier to talk to a guy than it is another woman."

Before he could examine Verona's expression too closely, she gave him another quick pat on the arm and headed out of the kitchen. He guessed the aftermath of the storm had everyone out of sorts. With a mental shrug, he headed back outside, stopping at the truck to get his new pair of heavy work gloves.

As he began loading the truck with splintered timbers, broken bricks and the shattered remains of his home's contents, he couldn't stop thinking about Verona's request. Now that he thought about it, Elissa had been acting a little weird. At first he'd thought she'd just been getting used to having a houseguest, but was something else going on? Maybe it was just the shock of the storm damage to the nursery and she was beginning to adjust to the new reality. After all, she'd seemed like her old self last night.

He stopped to wipe the sweat from his forehead and glanced over at Verona's front porch. Their pie raid had been fun, maybe what they both needed to try to get back to some semblance of normal. Now that he stepped back and really thought about it, he realized that he'd felt more at peace eating that pie with her beneath the stars than he had in a long time. The sudden hope that she'd felt the same way surprised him, making him wonder if maybe they were both a bit out of whack. Or maybe he'd been out in the sun too long.

It took all day and four trips to the refuse center, but by the time night began to fall, Pete had his lot cleared down to the foundation of his former home. As he trudged his way into Verona's house, he met her heading out to her poker game, pies in hand.

"I just baked a fresh batch of cookies. You and Elissa have been working so hard I figured you both deserved a treat. One you don't have to steal."

Pete inhaled the wonderful scent of fresh-baked cookies. "Are those snickerdoodles?"

"Yes, I made your favorite. Tell me how wonderful I am."

He leaned over and planted a kiss on her cheek. "You're wonderful."

"I made some oatmeal chocolate chip cookies, too." Elissa's favorite.

"We should steal your pies more often if we get cookies as a reward."

Verona swatted him on the shoulder. "Don't get sassy." She gestured toward the hallway. "You better hop in the shower. We may not be the big city here, but I'm still pretty sure none of the restaurants in town are going to let you in smelling like you do."

"Ouch," he said, feigning hurt.

"Well, you are a little ripe, definitely too stinky for a date."

A date? What was she talking about? Surely she didn't mean...

Verona headed for the door. "Well, I better get going. I plan to win myself a pile of money off those old ladies tonight." She smiled and winked at him. "Don't do anything I wouldn't do."

Even after Verona disappeared into the garage, Pete continued to stare at the door she'd closed behind her. Oh, hell, it wasn't Elissa or him who'd been knocked in the head. It was Verona, because damned if she wasn't in full-on matchmaking mode and had finally set her sights on her niece. The only problem was the guy Verona had in mind was him.

Chapter Five

When Elissa got home from a long, frustrating day of work, she arrived to find an empty house. Verona was off at her poker game, and Pete was absent, as well. Part of her was glad for the peace and quiet, but it also meant she was going to have to scrounge up her own dinner. And she didn't know if she had the energy.

Her stomach grumbled when she stepped into the kitchen and inhaled the scent of freshly baked cookies. Maybe she'd just have cookies for dinner. That didn't sound half-bad, not to mention blessedly easy. She found enough energy to pour herself a cold glass of milk and grab a handful of cookies before she headed for the living room. She sank onto one end of the cushy couch, kicked off her sneakers and propped her aching feet on the ottoman.

She took a bite of a cookie and closed her eyes in appreciation. There wasn't a better comfort food than oatmeal chocolate chip cookies. After she'd downed three cookies and the entire glass of milk, she let her head drop against the back of the couch and closed her eyes. The longer she sat, the more her body relaxed. She really needed to drag her tired butt to the shower, but she couldn't scrape up enough energy.

Elissa was drifting close to sleep when the door opening startled her awake. She blinked several times to clear her vision, then glanced toward the kitchen to see Pete walking through the doorway carrying two pizza boxes from Gino's and a couple of sodas.

"Hope those aren't both for you," she said.

A momentary odd expression passed over his face before he walked toward her. "That depends. What will you give me for a slice of pepperoni?"

"How about I promise not to leave a lizard in your bed?" For a guy who toted a gun and had chased down his share of criminals, he hated lizards with a maddening passion.

He narrowed his eyes at her. "Just for that, I ought to take these down to the music hall and make them first come, first served."

"But you won't because I'm going to now do my best to look pitiful and make you feel sorry for me." She pulled an exaggerated pout.

Pete rolled his eyes at her before stepping over her legs and plopping down on the couch beside her.

She smiled and batted her eyes at him. "I knew it would work."

"You do look pretty pitiful."

She swatted him on the arm before nabbing a big slice of pepperoni. After swallowing a bite, she glanced back at him. "I noticed you didn't take it easy on your day off."

"Nope, it needed doing." He sounded distracted.

"What's wrong?"

He glanced at her as if only suddenly realizing she was there. "Nothing, why?"

"I don't know. You sound...off."

He shrugged as he pulled another slice of pizza out of the box and then clicked on the TV. "Tired, I guess."

"No, that's not it."

He looked at her more fully this time and raised an eyebrow. "You're a mind reader now?"

"I don't have to be to know you're not telling me the truth."

"I am tired, and so are you. So let's just chill, okay?"

"Whatever." She shifted her attention to the TV and watched as Pete flipped channels. By the time he started on the third round through the offerings, she couldn't stand it and stole the remote from him. "God, guys are so irritating with these things. Pick something and stick with it." She flipped until she found an episode of *Hawaii Five-0*.

"Haven't you seen this one already?"

"Yeah. And your point?"

"That you've seen it already."

"And Alex O'Loughlin isn't any less hot on the third viewing."

"Great. Thanks for that image in my head."

"What? Like you've never watched something just because there was a hot girl in it."

"Not when I'm with you, or any other woman."

"Yeah, well, my house. And I'm going to watch hot cops."

"I'm a cop."

She looked toward him, wondering if she'd heard what she thought she had. But Pete was shoving another piece of pizza in his mouth and staring at the TV. No, she must have imagined it. Damn, she thought she'd gotten past her little infatuation, but evidently not judging from the way her heart had leapt at what she'd imagined he'd said.

Her crazy brain had manufactured not only the response but the tone as well, as if Pete wanted her to look at him the way she looked at McGarrett and the gang.

With a mental shake of her head, she refocused on her dinner. After a few minutes of Pete's cop commentary on the show, she was ready to slug him.

"Remind me not to watch cop shows with you ever again," she said.

After the program went off, she tossed the remote into his lap and had every intention of heading for the shower. But she couldn't force herself to rise. Instead, she sank deeper into the couch and let herself get caught up in *The Fellowship of the Ring.* It was the part where Frodo and the rest of the fellowship were in Rivendell.

"I want to live there," Elissa said.

"You just like the elf dudes."

"That would be a nice bonus." But what she really liked was how beautiful and peaceful it looked, ethereal. "That's one place I've never been."

"Pretty sure no one has been to Rivendell."

She tossed her balled-up napkin at him. "New Zealand, you goob."

"I thought you'd been just about everywhere with your parents."

With a travel-writer mother and an arts-dealer father, she had been all over the world until she'd decided to live a normal high school existence with her aunt. "Lots of locales, but not all. The world's a big place."

"Maybe I should go see some of it before the next tornado blows me away," he said.

She gave him a stern look. "Don't joke about that."

He seemed surprised by her vehemence. In truth, she was, too. But every time she thought about how close he'd come to dying, it hurt her heart. And a voice deep inside her whispered that it was more than friendship talking.

She pulled her gaze away from him and refocused on the movie. She sensed that he watched her for a few more seconds before he also returned his attention to the TV screen. Her common sense yelled at her to get up, to leave the room, but it was as if she'd used up the last of the day's worth of mobility just getting to the couch in the first place. Her eyes started growing heavy as the movie's atmospheric music lulled her to relax even more. Maybe she'd just sleep here and Pete would eventually leave.

"Elissa."

Was someone saying her name? It seemed so soft, so far away. She moved toward the sound and tried to open her eyes but couldn't. But that was okay. She was safe where she was, and whoever was calling her would still be there when she woke up.

PETE STARTED TO reach for Elissa, where she'd snuggled against his arm, to wake her up, but the look on her face stopped him. She looked relaxed, an expression he hadn't seen on her since before the storm. He wasn't the only one who'd worked himself to exhaustion today, and Elissa deserved to rest even if that meant he couldn't.

Chances were she'd wake up in a few minutes and make her way to her bedroom. Until then, he'd just focus on the movie and not on the feel of her warm cheek against his upper arm. Or on the fact that her aunt had evidently gotten the crazy idea into her head to push the two of them together. If Elissa knew, she'd have a fit. But he wasn't about to point it out to her and make everything awkward when he was still staying in her guest room.

He fought sleep as long as he could but felt himself

starting to drift when Elissa shifted against him. Before he could pull himself fully awake, Elissa had shifted to where her head was lying against his leg. He froze, unsure what to do. If she woke up now, they'd both be embarrassed. Could he slide out from under her without waking her so she'd never know what she'd done? He tried, but as soon as he moved she shifted again and placed her hand on his leg as she might her pillow.

His breath caught when his body reacted in a very uncomfortable way, a way that it shouldn't react to Elissa. He closed his eyes and let his breath out slowly, but it did nothing to alleviate his unexpected state. Hell, he should have woken her up when she'd first started drifting off. Better yet, he should have gone out to the Frothy Stein for a drink instead of bringing pizza back to the house. But that damn hindsight was frustratingly twenty-twenty.

Even though a voice in his head told him he shouldn't, he let his gaze wander to her face. A lock of her hair lay across her cheek, and before he could think better of it he reached to push it back behind her ear. When his fingers grazed across her skin, he realized he'd never touched her face. She wasn't a dainty flower of a woman, so the smooth softness of her cheek surprised him. He didn't know what he'd expected, but the tender feeling that brief touch caused wasn't it.

His thoughts careened back several years, to that hot August day when he'd seen her for the first time as they'd been beginning their freshman year of high school. He'd thought her the most beautiful girl he'd ever seen. Tall with long dark hair and an infectious smile, and she'd been to so many interesting places. His only forays out of the country had been two weekend trips to Mexico. She'd been new, exotic, and he'd fallen instantly and hard.

But over time, his undying love had faded the way high school crushes usually did. Instead, they'd become good friends, and until this moment that had been enough. Now his thoughts were drifting into dangerous territory. The stories of friends who'd tried to be more only to ruin the friendship were legion, and he wasn't willing to risk it over what might only be a case of hormones and too long a dry spell.

He needed to round up a date, and fast.

But for now, he couldn't stop looking at Elissa while it was safe. She'd never know.

He shook his head. What was he doing? He let his head drop back against the couch and closed his eyes. To keep dangerous thoughts out of his head, he forced himself to think of other things. His need to find a new place to live, his work schedule for the rest of the week, the price of a cup of coffee at the Primrose Café. Anything and everything but the feel of his friend's soft cheek against his leg.

ELISSA CAME AWAKE slowly and snuggled into the warmth of her bed. But when she tried to turn over, something didn't seem right. As she opened her eyes, the cogs in her head clicked through a couple more turns. She gasped and jerked upright when she realized where she was, waking Pete in the process.

"What's wrong?" he said as he pushed the upper half of his body up off the couch.

Elissa noticed that not only had they both fallen asleep, but somehow they'd also ended up lying down with a quilt draped over them. And early morning light was filtering in through the windows. Turning away from him, she extricated herself from the quilt and stood.

"Sorry, I didn't mean to fall asleep."

Pete tossed the quilt aside and dropped his feet to the floor. "Me, neither."

Elissa brushed her hair out of her face and resisted running from the room as if she'd done something wrong. Nothing had happened, even if she did wake up snuggled against one of her best friends. The one she'd been having unwise feelings toward.

"Good morning." Verona's chipper voice startled Elissa. "Would you two like some coffee? I've just brewed a fresh pot."

Oh, hell. Their situation was growing more awkward by the moment. And the too-happy look on her aunt's face rubbed Elissa the wrong way. After some quick mental aerobics, Elissa decided the best course was to act as if nothing out of the ordinary was going on.

"Sounds good, but the shower is calling my name first. I'm still wearing yesterday's workday." Before Verona or Pete could say anything in response, Elissa headed toward the bathroom at what felt like an excruciatingly normal pace. But she was determined to not give any indication that she was freaked out by sleeping on the couch with Pete. She would act as if it were no weirder than if she, India and Skyler had had a slumber party and all crashed out on the couch together.

Once she was out of their sight, safe behind the bathroom door, she closed her eyes and let out a slow breath. Falling asleep on the couch with Pete was one thing. How had she ended up curled up next to him, using his arm as a pillow? Why hadn't he gone to bed after she fell asleep? Had he conked out right after her? The clean lot next door indicated he'd had just as busy and tiring a day as she had.

She shook her head and shucked her dirty clothes.

Maybe a warm shower would calm her racing thoughts and she'd emerge from the bathroom to find things weren't as awkward as they felt right now. Yeah, right.

By the time she finished showering, her heart rate hadn't slowed any. Why was she so freaked out? It wasn't as if they'd done anything. They hadn't even kissed, though she could now kick herself for letting that image form in her head. She shouldn't be thinking that way about someone she'd known since he'd been a gangly fifteen-year-old.

Well, he wasn't gangly or fifteen anymore, was he? No, here in the safety of her steamy bathroom, she could admit to herself that the man she'd awakened next to had filled out nicely. And if she stripped away the freaking out, it had actually felt oddly nice to have that warmth and firmness next to her.

She cursed under her breath. These kinds of thoughts were stupid because they weren't going anywhere. They were buddies, nothing more. Not to mention she was quite happy with her casual dating lifestyle, and Pete, while he dated, too, was going to eventually be one of those settle-down-and-have-two-point-five-kids sorts of guys.

After taking a deep breath, she opened the door and headed for her room to get dressed. She waited until she heard Pete close himself in the bathroom before she emerged and headed for the kitchen, determined not to even acknowledge she was aware of Verona's plan. She'd already told her not to go down that road. So if Verona persisted, Elissa was just going to pretend she didn't notice until her aunt gave up and refocused her match-making efforts elsewhere. There were plenty of other unattached people in town she could drive up the wall.

When she entered the kitchen, she headed straight

for the coffeepot. She filled her thermal bottle and then nabbed a couple of the oatmeal cookies.

"You need something a little healthier than cookies for breakfast," Verona said as she emerged from the laundry room at the opposite end of the kitchen.

"I'll grab something on the way to work."

"I don't mind making breakfast for you and Pete."

Elissa didn't miss the hopeful note in Verona's voice, but she didn't let it show. She nodded toward the bathroom. "You'll have to ask Pete if he wants anything. I've got to get cracking."

"You two looked so cozy when I came home last night."

Elissa gave a little snort of a laugh. "I was so tired I probably could have slept on the driveway." She took a big bite of a cookie and headed for the door. "Later."

As she made her escape to the garage, Elissa was already planning ways to stay out late. She needed to keep away from Verona until her jittery feelings regarding Pete went away. She needed to be able to say with absolute certainty that she wasn't interested in her friend romantically, and if she lied, even a little bit, she was afraid her aunt would know. And then that particular runaway train would be impossible to stop.

"PETE."

The sound of Anne Marie's voice jerked Pete from his wandering thoughts. He realized when he looked at her standing in the doorway to the 911 dispatch room that she'd obviously called to him more than once. "Sorry, what?"

"I said there's a wreck out on Gilbert Station Road

where it meets up with Buckner Lane. Where were you anyway? Because it sure wasn't here."

Back on the couch with Elissa curled up next to him. But he wasn't about to spill that truth to Anne Marie, or anyone else for that matter. Especially when he was damn confused about how it had felt to wake up with the realization that they'd spent the entire night nestled together on the couch.

He shoved the thoughts aside as he stood but refused to meet Anne Marie's gaze. "Got it." He grabbed his new hat off the edge of his desk and headed out the door.

But as he drove out of town, his mind shifted back to that morning, to how Elissa had jumped off the couch as if she'd been burned. Did she think he'd deliberately wrapped her in his arms? Surely she wouldn't think that when they'd been friends for so long.

He rubbed his forehead, trying to prevent the headache he had from getting worse. If he acted normally, things would be fine. Of course, it would help if he could forget that moment when a part of him had wanted to pull her even closer. He told himself that was nothing more than the involuntary response a guy was bound to have when he woke up with a female body snug against him. But a little voice at the back of his brain whispered that he was lying to himself, that maybe he had been without realizing it for a long time.

"Hell." Just what he needed when he was sleeping in the next room. He had to find a new place, and soon.

When he reached the intersection where a pickup truck had crunched the front passenger side of a small car, he refocused on his job. But when he stepped out of his patrol car, he recognized the car just before he heard the ambulance siren behind him.

He hurried to the open driver's door to find India sitting with her feet on the pavement and the airbag deflated. Pete dropped to one knee in front of her. "Are you okay?"

She nodded. "I think so, but…" She placed her hand on her stomach. "I've got to make sure the baby is okay."

"I'm sorry. I didn't see her. The sun was in my eyes."

Pete glanced up at a man he didn't recognize, evidently the driver of the pickup. "Sir, are you injured?"

The guy shook his head. "I'm fine. Is she okay?" Worry filled his expression and his shaky voice.

"If you'll go wait by your truck, I'll be with you in a minute." Pete refocused his attention on India. "The ambulance is almost here. Have you called Liam?"

She shook her head. "No. I don't want to scare him if nothing is wrong. And he's in Fort Worth today anyway."

The ambulance stopped behind his car, and the paramedics hopped out and headed toward them. One came to stand next to Pete while the other approached the driver of the truck.

While the paramedics checked over India and the guy, Pete took down the details of the accident and called Greg Bozeman to come tow in India's car. As one of the paramedics led India to the ambulance, India grabbed Pete's arm.

"I was on my way to the nursery. Go tell Elissa what happened, but tell her I'm okay."

"Don't worry," he said. "I'll take care of it."

After the ambulance took off with India, Pete moved to take the other driver's statement. After Pete was finished, the guy drove away in his barely damaged truck and Greg towed India's car. Pete was left with no choice but to go to the nursery to see Elissa. Sure, he could call her, but after everything she'd been through lately, this kind of news was best delivered in person. He refused to acknowledge that he might want to see her, too. All the way to the nursery, he kept telling himself he was just doing his job. If it was anything else, it was simply that he wanted to assure himself that their awkwardness from that morning was only a product of surprise and that all was back to normal between them.

He found her on a ladder, scraping broken pottery on a set of shelves into a plastic tote. When she noticed him, her eyes widened a fraction.

"Oh, hey. What are you doing out here?"

"Would you believe playing a game of human telephone?"

She scrunched her forehead. "Huh?"

"Listen, everything is okay, but India wanted me to tell you that she was in an accident on the way here."

"What?" Elissa jerked so much that the ladder shook.

Pete stepped forward to steady the ladder. "I said everything's okay."

"You also said my pregnant friend was just in a car accident." Elissa hurried down the ladder and tossed the tote to the ground, breaking the pottery even more.

"She seemed okay. Her car's pretty banged up, but she walked to the ambulance by herself."

"Ambulance?" Elissa headed for the door.

Pete followed, and grabbed her arm. "Come on, I'll drive you."

"I can drive myself."

He stared hard at her. "And I know you. You're going to exceed the speed limit by enough to cause another wreck."

"I won't speed."

He didn't believe her, so he followed her all the way to town. "I thought you said you weren't going to speed," he said as he got out of his car behind where she'd parked.

"I didn't."

"You went at least five miles per hour over all the way here."

"That's because all the speed limits are set five miles per hour too slow, and you know it."

Damn, he couldn't even argue with that because it was true. Still, he didn't like the idea of her going too fast and getting in an accident. He stopped in his tracks, letting her continue on into the hospital without him. His heart rate kicked up a notch as he watched her walk away and considered the thoughts that had just shot through his brain. When had he ever worried about how fast Elissa drove?

The answer was never. At least not until he'd moved into her house, not until he'd awakened with her next to him, making him want things he had no right to want.

Chapter Six

Elissa looked across the table in India's boutique the next morning. "Are you sure you're okay? Should you be working today?"

"I'm fine, really. I swear, between you and Liam, you'd think I was made of blown glass."

"I can't help it. You pregnant ladies keep getting toted off to the hospital and scaring me half to death." She glanced at Skyler, remembering when she'd fallen outside her inn the night of India's wedding.

"It's not like we do it on purpose to stress you out," Skyler said.

"I know." Elissa shook her head. "Hell, I'm just at my wits' end, and I don't like feeling this way." It wasn't like her, not in the least.

"Is something wrong?" India asked.

Elissa opened her mouth and almost confessed to her odd feelings about Pete, but she caught the words just in time. The last thing she needed was for her two best girlfriends, both of whom were crazy in love with their guys, to jump on Verona's bandwagon.

Instead, she sat back in her chair. "Just waiting to hear about the insurance settlement, and watching my bank account dwindle more every day that I have to be closed."

India reached across the table and squeezed her hand. "You'll get through this. Nothing gets Elissa Mason down for long."

Elissa tapped the top of the table with her knuckles. "You know, you're right. I'm not letting a tornado mess with me."

Now, an infatuation with her best guy friend might be a different story.

They quickly got through the final details on the next day's BlueBelles class on community volunteerism. The regular enrichment classes they held for local girls were always popular. But in the wake of the storm and the announcement that the class would involve hands-on volunteer work, all fifteen slots had filled up with girls ages nine to sixteen. India, Skyler and Elissa planned to open the class together and then split the girls into three work groups to tackle different jobs.

India closed the file folder on the table in front of her. "Okay, now that we've got that out of the way, let's move on to the rodeo. I saw Merline Teague this morning, and she had a great idea. In addition to the normal food vendors, she suggested we have a community-wide flea market. Give everyone space at the fairgrounds, and they can get rid of stuff they don't want and donate the proceeds to the recovery efforts."

Elissa started to comment but stopped when the front door opened to reveal Pete. He glanced at her briefly before shifting his attention to India. What was that about? Had he been as freaked out by their waking up together as she'd been? He hadn't acted as if anything was out of the ordinary the day before, but then the only time she'd seen him once she'd left the house was when he'd come to tell her about India's wreck. That hadn't exactly been the time to be dwelling on accidental sleeping partners.

"Hey, Pete," India said.

"Sorry to bother you all. I just stopped by to see how you're doing."

"Fine. Doctor says I'm perfectly healthy, which is more than I can say for my poor car."

"Cars can be replaced."

"True. Come on in. I have some fresh lemonade."

Elissa figured he'd decline, but he instead closed the door behind him and leaned against the front counter. Had he always been that tall? Been just as hot as any of the other cowboys who rolled into town for the regular rodeos? And why had she never realized how good he looked in his uniform, complemented by his new boots and hat?

Good grief, she had to get a hold on her whacked-out feelings.

"Lemonade sounds good about right now," Pete said. "I've spent the morning directing traffic while they pave the highway north of town."

"The glamorous work of Blue Falls' finest," Skyler said with a laugh.

Pete smiled a little, but Elissa caught a hint of something else. If she had to say what, she'd go with frustration. Then again, she wouldn't be too up on life if she had to stand out in the middle of a hot Texas highway playing traffic light, either.

India poured Pete a glass of cold lemonade and handed it over. After he took a big gulp, he looked back toward where they sat.

"What are you all working on?"

"The rodeo," India said. "This one wasn't planned out

too far in advance, so we're sort of scrambling to make sure we get a lot of riders. Hey, you used to team-rope. You want to come out of retirement?"

"You must really be desperate if you're asking me to take part."

"I wouldn't say desperate exactly. You were good."

Pete laughed. "*Were* being the operative word. But sure, I'll call Charlie and see if he's up for it. Who knows, maybe I'll win enough to buy myself a refrigerator box to live in."

Pete was joking, but something about what he said made Elissa's heart hurt. Why had she been focusing on stupid things like where she'd fallen asleep and how Pete looked without a shirt when there were so many bigger, more important things to think about?

She glanced at the clock on the wall and was surprised by the time. "I've got to run. I'm meeting the contractor to get an estimate on the rebuild, and find out just how old I'm going to be when I finally get my debt paid off."

"I better get back to work, too," Pete said. "No telling what exciting things the afternoon holds for me."

Elissa glanced up just in time to see a look pass between India and Skyler. Warning bells went off in her head, but she couldn't exactly question them about it with Pete standing only a few feet away. Which was probably a good thing considering her plan to ignore any and all matchmaking efforts until they went away.

Pete opened the door and held it for Elissa. He'd probably done that a million times, but she got the oddest sensation that India and Skyler were watching his action with a new interest. She gritted her teeth in frustration. How had she managed to let this happen? Until now, she'd been a master at steering Verona's Cupid ways in other directions. But her aunt had caught her distracted and launched her attack. She didn't know if she'd enlisted Skyler and India or if somehow she herself had unconsciously hinted that there was a flicker of interest toward Pete.

She couldn't think about this now. If she did, her head might explode.

"You okay?" Pete asked as he walked beside her down the sidewalk.

"Yeah. Just busy and tired, the norm of late."

When she glanced at him, he looked as if he wanted to say something else. Afraid of what it might be and not wanting to deal with it right now, she stepped off the sidewalk toward her SUV. "See ya later. Loads to do."

She didn't give him a chance to respond before she opened the door and hopped inside. She tossed a wave his way without really looking at him as she pulled away from the curb, hoping to leave her confusing feelings on that sidewalk right beside Pete.

HALFWAY THROUGH THE afternoon, Pete realized he'd been staring at the same thing on his computer for so long his eyes were burning. He'd been in this same situation before. Well, maybe not exactly the same. The last time he'd been on the verge of filling out the application to the state police academy, he wasn't homeless. No, he'd thought he'd finally gotten to a point in his life where he could take the first necessary step toward his dream of becoming a Texas Ranger like his dad before him.

But then his mother's cancer had returned, and he'd had to put that dream on hold. As he stared at the application now, he almost felt as if something awful would happen if he filled it out. That was stupid, of course.

What else could he possibly lose? He had no family left, no home.

You could lose Elissa.

She wasn't his to lose.

He ran his hand over his face and back through his hair. Ever since he'd awakened on that couch with her pressed against him, he couldn't get how it had felt out of his head. It was wrong, but he'd kept replaying it in his mind, wondering what might have happened if Elissa hadn't leapt away from him, if they'd been alone.

Nothing, that's what. Elissa's reaction was the one that made sense, and he needed to shove the entire incident out of his mind. And he had to get out of her house before he did or said something he'd regret, something that would ruin a friendship he wanted to keep.

He'd start asking around about a place to rent. Once they had some distance between them, things would most likely settle back to how they should be, how they'd been on the porch when they were eating pie.

He tapped his knuckles on the top of his desk a couple of times, took a deep breath and started filling out the application. He tried not to think about how he'd have to leave Blue Falls if he got into the academy. It was what he'd always wanted. Heck, Elissa knew that. She was the one who'd encouraged him to apply the first time.

But as he typed in the information, he couldn't help the ache that settled inside him right alongside the excitement and hope that maybe he was finally going to take that first step toward what he'd wanted since he was a boy who'd worshipped his dad.

ELISSA BACKED UP Pete's truck so that her group of Blue-Belles girls could load the debris they'd collected from around Agnes Summers's house. When she'd asked Pete to trade vehicles for the day, he'd agreed and acted as if nothing was out of the ordinary. It was as if their awkward sleeping arrangement had never happened.

Why was she dwelling on that? Wasn't that what she wanted, for it to just go away, to not be any big deal? But there was some little bit of her that whispered that she did want it to mean something, no matter how insane that was.

No, she was simply off her game, she told herself as she slipped out of the truck. She'd spent so much time working and worrying lately that she didn't even feel like herself. But how was she supposed to get back to any sense of normalcy when her entire life was turned on its head? When she felt as if she was thinking with someone else's brain?

"Here, honey. You look as if you could use this." Mrs. Summers offered Elissa a cold Coke in one of those little bottles and a bottle opener to pop off the lid.

"Thanks, Mrs. Summers."

"Hon, you haven't had me in class in years. Call me Agnes."

"I'm not sure if I can. It feels weird." Mrs. Summers had been Elissa's freshman English teacher during her last year before retirement.

"Sure you can. Ag...nes. Say it with me."

Elissa laughed, and it felt good because it relieved some of the pressure she hadn't realized had been sitting on her chest like an elephant. "Okay, Agnes." She shook her head. "I still feel like I'm going to get sent to detention for saying that."

This time, Agnes laughed. "I never sent you to detention, even if you were one of the chattiest students I ever had."

"I had to make sure your last year was interesting."

Agnes smiled and looked out from beneath her wide-brimmed straw hat toward where the girls were tossing broken wooden fencing that had been around the small garden into the back of the truck.

"You've done a great job with these girls, with all of those classes you do."

"It's a group effort."

"Yes, and you're an integral part of that group." Agnes shifted her gaze back to Elissa. "You like to be the life of the party, but under all that laughter and teasing you've got a big heart."

Stunned by the compliment, Elissa didn't know what to say. "I'm just doing what any decent person would."

Agnes didn't respond, so Elissa started to step away.

"Are you happy?"

Elissa stopped and looked back at Agnes. "I'm sorry?"

"I taught for many, many years, and hundreds of kids went through my classroom. I got very good at spotting the ones who hid loneliness and pain behind humor."

Elissa scrunched her forehead, wondering if Agnes was beginning to get a little senile. That would be really sad. Or maybe…

"Have you been talking to Verona?"

This time, it was Agnes's turn to look confused before understanding dawned in her pale blue eyes. "Has she finally turned her matchmaking efforts toward you?"

Elissa sighed. "So it seems."

Agnes chuckled. "She is determined. She would probably have made a mint if she'd opened a matchmaking service years ago."

"Lord, don't give her any ideas. It's bad enough when she does it for free."

Agnes laughed and patted Elissa's arm with her wrinkled hand. "It's not all bad. There's a lot to be said for finding your true love and having a long, happy life together. I wouldn't trade the years I had with Bill for anything."

Elissa experienced a pang in her heart at the sadness that passed over Agnes's face. She'd lost her husband of fifty years a couple of years ago. Elissa couldn't imagine sharing that many years with someone and then one day he was just gone.

Agnes seemed to push her sorrow away and smiled. "I didn't mean to pry, dear." She took one of Elissa's hands between hers and squeezed gently. "I just like to see good people happy, and you're one of the sweetest girls I know. A live wire, no doubt, but sweet nonetheless."

Elissa didn't know how to respond, and Agnes gave her an out as she nodded and moved away to offer the girls something to drink.

Still, even after the job was done and Elissa had delivered the girls back to their parents, she couldn't stop thinking about what Agnes had said. Until the storm hit, she would have answered the "Are you happy?" question with an unequivocal yes. But since, nothing seemed quite so certain and simple anymore.

As she drove back through town, she noticed her SUV parked in front of the hardware store. As she maneuvered into a spot on the opposite side of the street, she spotted Pete stepping out of the store along with Charlie Parsons. She hurried across the street, wanting access to her own vehicle.

"Hey, Elissa," Charlie said as he spotted her.

"Charlie. Long time no see."

"Yeah, keeping busy. Even more so thanks to the storm."

"You have damage out at your place?"

"Yeah, some fencing down. Took me an entire day just to round up the cattle that decided to wander out and see the wider world."

Elissa smiled at the image of a massive cattle jailbreak. "Luckily, it wasn't horses. At least cows just tend to meander instead of making a run for it."

"True."

"You want your car back?" Pete said, drawing her attention for the first time.

She held up his keys. "You read my mind." She eyed the armful of lumber he was holding. "You get recruited to help out?"

Pete shot a glance at Charlie. "The price of him agreeing to rope with me at the rodeo."

Despite the awkward feelings she was doing her best to ignore, she laughed a little, then met Charlie's gaze. "Nicely played."

"I thought so," he said. "You know, we could use another set of hands."

"You're good, but not that good. I got plenty of my own to do."

But after swapping keys and vehicles with Pete, she didn't head to the nursery. Well, she got part of the way there before pulling over on the side of the road. The combination of stress, confusion about Pete and Agnes's words about finding love had her mind spinning. The last thing she wanted was to go face the destruction at the nursery again. After all, she'd already put in a full day with the BlueBelles class. She'd been acting like a different person since the storm, and it was time to reclaim the real Elissa Mason, the one who liked to go out and have a good time.

But instead of calling her friends for a girls' night, she hurried home to shower and change, then drove to Austin on her own. Despite the fact that she was losing money every day the nursery was closed, she engaged in some retail therapy anyway. One cute outfit and a kick-ass pair of shoes later, she headed for the theater and made herself comfortable with a big tub of buttery popcorn for not one but two new movies.

By the time she got out of the second movie, she was starving. After a quick stop by the Whataburger for a big, juicy hamburger and a milk shake, she headed home feeling more like herself than she had in days.

That peaceful normality evaporated when she pulled into her driveway and noticed Verona's car wasn't there. She hurried inside the house to find Pete stretched out along the couch asleep. She stopped in her tracks and stared for several seconds, realizing just how close they must have been to each other to have shared that small space. As it was, Pete seemed to cover it all by himself.

She came back to her senses and crossed the room. "Hey, Pete," she said as she swatted one of his booted feet. "Wake up."

He seemed disoriented for several seconds. "Oh, there you are."

"Where's Verona?"

That question seemed to wake him up more, and he lifted himself to a sitting position. "At Annabeth's. She had a heart scare earlier. The doc said she's okay, but Verona wanted to spend the night with her tonight just in case."

The rest of Elissa's good mood evaporated, replaced by guilt that she'd been out having a good time while Annabeth was at the hospital, fearing she might be having another heart attack.

"Don't worry," Pete said. "Verona said they did a whole battery of tests, and there was no indication of any cardiac problems."

Elissa sank onto the arm of the chair adjacent to the couch. "She's really careful about her health since she had her heart attack. I think sometimes she just gets nervous and freaks herself out."

"That's the impression I got from Verona."

Elissa slid into the chair, resting her back against the opposite arm. "Did you get Charlie's fence repaired today?"

"Yeah. I think the cows were giving us the evil eye, too."

Elissa laughed at that mental image.

"I was going to come out and lend a hand at the nursery, but Verona said you'd gone to Austin."

"Yeah, just needed to get away for a while, try to remember what life was like before I worked every minute of every day."

"Have you heard from the insurance company yet?"

"No, and it's driving me batty. I think I'm going to have to get started with repairs before I get the check."

"Maybe you'll get it soon. I received mine today."

"That's good. So you going to start rebuilding?"

He pecked the edge of the coffee table with his knuckles. "Depends."

"On?"

He met her gaze. "On if I get into the academy."

Her breath caught in her chest, and that told her more

than anything that her feelings toward her friend had changed. "You applied again?"

"Yeah. Nothing really holding me here anymore. Seemed like the time."

Elissa did her best not to react because she knew how much this meant to him, how he'd always wanted to follow in his father's footsteps and become a Texas Ranger. After everything he'd been through, he deserved to finally be able to chase his dream. That didn't mean she couldn't fear for his safety. Sure, he could be hurt at work now or could fall off his horse and break his neck while out riding, but she had to believe both of those possibilities were statistically less likely. But she would never voice her concerns like his mother had. His mother's fear hadn't been without reason. After all, she'd lost her husband to the same career her only child wanted to pursue.

But his mother wasn't here now. Neither was Pete's home. Elissa couldn't expect her friendship and his position at the sheriff's department to be enough to keep him in Blue Falls. And she wouldn't admit to any feelings that might change his mind.

"That's great." She forced a smile. "If they're smart, they'll snatch you up."

When he gave a little smile back, her heart performed a strange flip that left her momentarily dizzy and thankful she was sitting down.

"I'll start looking for a place to rent tomorrow."

"There's no hurry." Earlier, she would probably have welcomed having normality return to her house, but with the possibility that he might be moving away she found herself not so eager to have him vacate her guest room. "If you'll be heading to the academy soon, doesn't make much sense to rent a place here."

"There's no guarantee I'll get in, and I've been intruding long enough."

"You'll get in, and you're not intruding."

"Are you sure?" The look he gave her made her wonder if she'd been more obvious about her changing feelings than she'd thought.

She waved away his concern with a sound that made it obvious he was being silly. "Of course I'm sure. Though I might start making you take out the garbage."

"Oh, that settles it. I'm definitely moving out."

Elissa threw a pillow at him and laughed, thankful for the familiar, friendly banter.

She just hoped she could maintain it until either her little infatuation dissipated or Pete moved away.

If she were honest with herself, she didn't think the first was going to happen. And the second option, well, she couldn't think about that right now. Before her facade cracked, she stood.

"I'm hitting the hay so I can go back to the real world tomorrow." She headed for her room. "Oh, and don't forget tomorrow is garbage day."

She glanced toward him just in time to dodge the pillow he sent flying her way.

Chapter Seven

Pete walked in to work the next afternoon to find Connor Murphy waiting for him.

"What did I do?" Pete asked.

"It's not what you did but what you're going to do—a favor for your good buddy."

"Why am I afraid to ask?"

"It's not a favor for me, really. Actually, think about it as me doing you a favor."

Pete gave Connor a raised-eyebrow look.

"Okay, listen. I need you to be my cousin Leah's date to the dance after the rodeo. She just called and said she's coming for a visit from Corpus. She's a jewelry maker, and she's going to set up a booth at the flea market and donate part of the proceeds to the tornado victims fund. So I can't exactly say no."

"I thought you liked Leah." She was an artsy type, but she'd always been fun from what Pete remembered.

"I do, but that's the night I'm going out with Kristi McKee. Took me two months to get her to say yes."

Pete's thoughts went to Elissa, but she'd seemed like her old self last night. Whatever he'd thought might have been there obviously wasn't, and he kept telling himself he should be glad. The last thing he needed to do was screw up a good friendship.

He shrugged. "Sure. Don't have to twist my arm to get me to go out with a pretty girl."

"I owe you, man."

"I'll remember that the next time I draw a morning shift."

He'd only been in the office a few minutes when he got a domestic call and headed out to the far edge of the county. He hated these kinds of calls more than anything not involving a dead body. An hour later, he shook his head as he and Simon Teague led not only the husband but also the wife to two separate patrol cars in cuffs.

Once both parties were safely tucked away, Pete shook his head. "Ever feel like our species is getting dumber by the minute?"

"All the time. I count myself lucky that if I make Keri mad, all she does is make me mop the floor or something."

"I guess taking out the garbage isn't so bad."

What the hell? Why had he said that? Simon gave him an odd look, and Pete found himself scrambling for a response that didn't reveal he'd been thinking about his friend in a very unfriendlike way lately, noticing how her T-shirt hugged her breasts, how her jeans fit her hips.

"It's better than paying rent. Verona and Elissa aren't bad landlords."

Simon eyed him in a way that made Pete suspect his boss wasn't fooled.

"Well, we better get these gems of the gene pool to lockup," Pete said, hoping to shift attention away from his slip.

On the drive back to Blue Falls, Pete got to listen to

the woman in the backseat call him a colorful array of names as she tried to convince him she'd done nothing wrong. Sure, her husband was a horse's ass and shouldn't have thrown a wrench at her, but that didn't mean she could use him as target practice using a dozen bottles of beer, either.

Pete rolled his eyes and stared at the road ahead. He would have been better off to focus on the tirade, because when he tuned her out, his thoughts shifted to Elissa. Until a few minutes ago, he hadn't realized just how often he'd thought about her lately. And how those thoughts had gradually shifted since he'd moved into her guest room. Was it just being in more frequent contact with a woman his own age? If he moved out, would those thoughts go away? Despite Elissa telling him he could stay as long as he liked, maybe he should step up his search for a place to rent. At least then he'd know whether he was losing his mind or not.

The image of her pushing her hair behind her ear popped into his mind. He'd seen her do that a million times, and yet now the image made his skin warm and his hands flex on the steering wheel. Why hadn't he noticed how beautiful she was before now?

That was a dumb question. He'd always known she was pretty, but she'd been Elissa, a close friend since before either of them could even drive. Why was that changing now? And was there any possibility that she was experiencing the same confusing feelings?

Pete ran his hand over his face. He couldn't risk asking her, not when it might ruin their friendship. And he just wasn't up for losing anything or anyone else right now. He'd had about enough loss to last a lifetime.

Miss Classy in the backseat banged on the cage divider keeping her from strangling him.

"Are you even listening to me?" she asked.

"Nope."

"I'm a taxpaying citizen, so you work for me."

He eyed her in the rearview mirror. "For what you pay, I was justified to stop listening about the time I slapped the cuffs on you."

She let loose with another string of cursing.

Pete ground his teeth. He hoped Elissa was right and he got into the state police academy. As he tried to block out his passenger's displeasure, he thought the acceptance letter couldn't come soon enough.

Except that he'd be leaving Elissa behind.

He cursed under his breath. As soon as he escorted his prisoner to her cell, he was going to look for a new place to lay his head at night before he made a complete and utter fool of himself.

THERE'S A CONTRACTOR here said you called him."

Elissa looked up from where she was boxing up a few plants she would donate to the flea market at the rodeo. Anderson Bell, one of her employees, gestured back over his shoulder toward the door.

"Okay, thanks." She wiped her hands on her jeans and headed outside. When she saw the man waiting for her, he wasn't a middle-aged guy with a little extra weight around the middle. Far from it.

Well, hello there, Mr. Hotness.

The guy was about her age, maybe a little older, with dark blond hair and a nice pair of tanned arms. His smile was enough to make any right-minded woman's toes curl.

"Ms. Mason?"

"Elissa, please," she said as she extended her hand.

"Brett Fenton." He took her hand in a nice, firm shake. "I believe you talked to my dad this morning about some construction work."

"I did." She let go of his hand and gestured behind her. "As you can see, the building has seen better days."

"I don't know. I think maybe it has character."

She laughed at his unexpected remark. "Little too much character, if you ask me."

He shrugged. "Maybe it does need a bit of a face-lift."

When he smiled at her again, she felt a little more normality slip back into place. "And how much is this face-lift going to cost me?"

"I'd love to do it for free, but I'm sure my dad would disinherit me."

She leaned toward him and faux-whispered, "I won't tell if you don't."

Brett laughed, and it was a nice laugh. "Let me look around and take some measurements so I can give you a quote."

She nodded and forced herself back toward the door when she really wanted to stay outside and check out what he looked like from the backside.

A twinge of something hit her middle, and her thoughts shifted to Pete. She was inside and halfway to the far back of the building before she identified the twinge as guilt. The shock of that stopped her in the middle of the aisle between stacks of birdseed and a shelf that had held decorative watering cans.

Why would she feel guilty for ogling a good-looking man? It certainly wasn't the first time she'd done so, and if she had her way it wouldn't be the last. She knew all too well that her two best friends had found their once-in-a-lifetime loves, but she actually liked being single, having the freedom to do what she wanted with who she wanted when she wanted.

An image of running her hands over Pete's naked chest formed in her mind, causing her neck and face to flush with heat.

"You okay?"

Elissa glanced over at where Anderson had come through the large, open doorway that led to the room where he was cleaning up the collapsed displays of gardening tools.

"Uh, yeah. Trying to decide what to do next." At least that's what she said. What she thought was entirely different—that she was going absolutely bananas. Seriously, how was she supposed to maintain her easy, casual friendship with Pete if she kept daydreaming about running her hands over his naked skin?

But it was such nice skin over very nice muscles.

Good grief!

She continued to the back of the building, the part that had received the least amount of damage from the tornado. Here she could almost believe her life hadn't been turned upside down, that her relationship with Pete hadn't taken an unexpected turn. For the first time in her life, she was attracted to someone she couldn't pursue. She took a deep breath, trying to figure out how to get past this ill-advised attraction.

Movement outside the window caught her attention. When she noticed it was Brett examining the exterior of the building, she latched on to the idea that maybe he was an attractive step back to her normal, fun-loving self.

She forced herself to get back to work until Brett

tracked her down about forty-five minutes later. "All finished?"

He nodded. "You want to go over these figures now or do you want me to just leave them with you?"

"I have another idea. Do you have to get back to Austin right away?"

The hint of a smile tugged at the edge of Brett's lips. "No, I actually have one more estimate to do in the area."

"Good, that's perfect timing. You like Mexican food?"

"Do I live in Texas?"

She smiled. "Then I think we should discuss the estimate over dinner at La Cantina. Any objection to that?"

"None at all." He gave her a look that backed up his words.

"You have a business card?"

The question seemed to catch him off guard, but he pulled one from his wallet anyway. She took it and wrote her address on the back before handing it back to him.

"I'll be ready by six-thirty."

Brett glanced at the card, then back at her. "I look forward to it."

As he walked away, she told herself she was looking forward to it, too. Even if a part of her mind was whispering that the man she wanted to spend tonight with wasn't Brett Fenton.

BY THE TIME Pete got off work and drove to Verona's, he was ready to chuck law enforcement altogether. That's what an afternoon of people behaving like idiots did to a guy. Maybe he'd take up professional fishing, or see if Glory needed help at the stables. At least then he could spend his workdays alone and not have to listen to the rantings of people who probably didn't have a dozen IQ points to their names.

When he stepped into the kitchen, he spotted Verona at the stove, flipping quesadillas.

She glanced up at him. "Hon, you look like you're wrung out."

"Been one of those days." Not only had he been inundated with stupid all day, but any moment he wasn't dealing with nitwits he was thinking about Elissa. He'd let himself imagine what it would have been like to be more than friends with her if they'd only just met and didn't have the years of friendship barring that path.

"Well, dinner will be ready in a couple of minutes."

"You know you don't have to cook for me every night."

"I gotta eat. Doesn't take that much effort to make a little extra."

"Can I help?"

"You can grab the sodas."

He headed for the fridge. "How's Annabeth?"

"Much better. She feels so silly when it turns out to be nothing."

"Better safe than sorry."

"That's what I told her." Verona looked toward him, noticed the drinks in his hands and let out a little sigh. "We only need two of those. Elissa's got a date tonight."

His gut reaction was not that of a friend. A friend wouldn't feel the sudden jealousy that plowed into him. Not good, not good at all.

"Oh, that's good. She deserves a night out."

"So do you, sweetie."

He forced a huff of a laugh. "Trust me, after the day I've had, I'm perfectly fine hiding from humanity for a while."

Just as he set the cold bottles of soda on the table, someone knocked on the front door.

"Could you get that?"

Pete glanced at Verona, and there was an odd light in her eyes, enough to tell him that she was up to something. Too tired and frustrated to try to figure out what it was, he headed for the door. He had the oddest urge to place his hand on his service weapon, to put the fear of God, or at least Elissa's law-enforcement houseguest, into whoever was at the door. He fought a smile that at least the guy would see his uniform and the gun on his hip.

The moment he opened the door, he pegged the guy as exactly the type Elissa always went for—tall, lanky, good-looking and maybe a touch too aware of all that. For a satisfying couple of seconds, the guy's eyes widened.

"Hey, I'm here to pick up Elissa for dinner."

Pete made him wait a moment more before he took a step back to let the guy in.

"Are you Elissa's brother?"

"No, best friend." He didn't know why he put that "best" in there. Oh, hell, yeah, he did. He wanted the guy to know that if he hurt Elissa in any way, he wouldn't be dealing with just the wrath of a woman and her girlfriends.

"Oh. I'm Brett Fenton."

"Pete Kayne. How did you two meet?"

"I'm hoping I'll be doing the reconstruction work at her nursery. We're going to talk over the estimate tonight."

So it was a working dinner. That made Pete feel a fraction better, at least until he turned and saw Elissa. The pink sleeveless dress and the way she had her dark hair down and loose definitely didn't say *working dinner.*

Damn, she took his breath away, no matter how dangerous it was for him to feel that way.

"Wow, you look beautiful," Brett said.

Yeah, she did, and Pete had the deep urge to punch Brett for saying so. But he didn't have the right, not unless Brett hurt Elissa. And God help him if he made that mistake.

Pete didn't realize how long he'd been staring at Elissa until her eyes shifted from her date to him. Her smile faltered a bit, and he realized he must be making her uncomfortable. He broke eye contact and took a step back. Even though he told himself not to, he couldn't help letting his gaze shift to her again. She gave him the hint of a smile before crossing the space between her and Brett.

"Shall we go? I hope you don't expect me to be one of those girls who eats like a bird."

Brett laughed, setting Pete's teeth on edge.

"Not at all." Brett gestured toward the front door, allowing Elissa to precede him.

Brett shifted his attention to Pete. "Nice meeting you, man."

A moment ticked by before Pete responded, "You, too." He hesitated a fraction of a second before adding, "Have a good time."

Brett nodded before following Elissa out the door.

Pete allowed himself to think up all kinds of reasons to justify arresting Brett. Unfortunately, all of them were complete hooey. Besides, he'd seen Elissa out on more dates than he could count. Seeing her head off on one more shouldn't bother him.

But it did.

Movement from the kitchen made him realize that Verona hadn't even emerged to meet Elissa's date. He also realized that he couldn't possibly sit down to dinner across from Verona, not when he wasn't in complete control of his feelings. Elissa's aunt would hop on that horse and ride it till it frothed at the mouth.

"I'm going to have to take a rain check on dinner," he said without meeting her gaze. "I remembered I didn't write a report I need to."

"It's no problem. I'll just save yours, and you can have it when you come back."

"Thanks, but I don't know when I'll be back."

"Must be one heck of a report."

He made the mistake of meeting her gaze and saw the doubt there. She didn't believe he was going to write an incident report any more than she believed the Spurs would move the team to Blue Falls. Unwilling to get into a discussion about why she was right, he strode toward the door and out into the gathering evening. But once he was outside, he stood in the driveway and wondered what in the heck he was going to do next.

ELISSA HANDED HER menu back to the waitress at La Cantina and shifted her attention to Brett to find him watching her with a smile tugging at his lips. "What?"

"Just thinking I wish all my days of doing estimates ended like this."

"By eating Mexican food? That might be hard on your waistline."

His smile widened. "No, sitting across from a beautiful woman."

"Why, thank you."

"Although I have to say it's the first time I've picked up a date and been greeted at the door by a guy with a gun."

"Now, why do I doubt that?"

He raised an eyebrow. "I think I'm offended."

She made a sound of dismissal. "No, you're not."

"You think you know me, do you?"

"I've been out with enough guys to know when one has a little streak of mischief in him."

"Has your best friend shot any of them?"

She was momentarily confused until she figured he must mean Pete. Was he just assuming they were best friends, or had Pete introduced himself that way? While a surge of warmth welled up inside her, it was accompanied by a twinge of unexpected sadness she couldn't explain.

"No, Pete's a good guy. He's staying with my aunt and me until he finds a new place. His house was destroyed in the tornado."

"Sorry to hear that."

For a moment, she wasn't sure if Brett was talking about Pete's house or the fact that he was sleeping in her guest room.

An awkward silence settled between them, something that had rarely ever happened to her on a date. But when she would normally be flirting, she found it hard to pull her thoughts away from Pete, from the fact that no matter what happened with the academy he would be moving out soon.

"Should we get the business out of the way so we can enjoy our dinner?" Brett asked.

"Yes." She tried to ignore how she jumped on that line of conversation like a life raft.

"The good news is a good portion of your building is still structurally sound."

"And the bad?"

He gave her an apologetic smile. "The parts that were

damaged are going to need significant work. In some parts, we'll have to totally rebuild from the ground up."

"And I'm guessing the worst news is the price tag."

"I won't lie and say it'll be cheap, but I can get started by the end of the week." He handed her the written estimate.

Elissa took a deep breath before looking at the paper, her eyes going immediately to the bottom line. The number punched her in the gut, twice what she had guessed it to be. "I'm thinking I should have let Pete shoot you."

"I know it's a shock, but the cost of materials have really gone up in the past year. I assume you'll get more estimates, but I honestly don't think they're going to be a lot different."

Of course he would say that, seeing as how he wanted her business and most likely a commitment from her tonight.

She read over every line in the estimate. "I think I went into the wrong business."

"No, I think you're in the right one. You know, my mom is quite a fan of shopping at your nursery."

She looked up at him. "Any chance if I call her she can convince you to halve this?"

"Sorry. It's the best I can do."

When she spotted the waitress bringing their food, Elissa folded the estimate and stuffed it in her purse. "Well, enough of that for now."

Throughout dinner, they talked about everything from the amount of destruction he'd seen while out doing estimates to her travels in Australia, somewhere he'd always wanted to go.

"I can't believe you gave up all that traveling to settle here."

"Why? You live in Texas."

He shrugged. "I don't know, something about how you describe all those places you've been. Maybe you inherited some of your mother's talent for description."

"I know it all seems glamorous, but there were times when I was sleeping in strange places when all I wanted was a bedroom of my own that I could plaster with posters of hot guys and to attend school somewhere I could go to Friday night football games."

Suddenly, an image of India, Skyler and her sitting on the bleachers at the high school football stadium popped into her mind. They were eating popcorn and watching classmates such as Greg Bozeman, the Teague brothers and Pete on the field. The image was so real she'd swear she could smell the hot, buttery popcorn and hear the band playing pep songs during time-outs.

"Yeah, I guess eating all that weird food would make you crave a cheeseburger."

She laughed and nodded. "True, though there were some places where the food was fantastic. Italy and France come to mind."

The rest of their dinner passed with them swapping more stories, but by the end of the meal Elissa found herself in an unusual position when sitting across from an attractive man. She just wanted to go home. When she would normally suggest heading to the music hall for some dancing, her thoughts went instead to her pajamas and some time alone to figure out how she was going to pay for the repairs she had no choice but to make. If she just had her insurance check in hand, she'd at least feel a little better. Of course, she was still going to be a great-grandmother before she paid off everything.

Hard to be a great-grandmother when you didn't even have kids. Or a husband.

Her breath caught when her mind produced a picture of Pete.

"Are you okay?"

She refocused her attention on Brett. "Yeah." The way he looked at her, she felt as if she needed to say something else but she came up empty.

"Well, it's been a long day for both of us. I should get you home. Plus, don't want your friend to think I've kept you out too late." He smiled, and there was something about that smile she couldn't decipher. It was almost as if he knew something but was keeping it to himself.

Or maybe the combination of tiredness and worry over paying for the repairs had her imagining things.

Who was she kidding? She'd been off her game ever since the night of the storm. Ever since she'd seen Pete's naked chest and started having inappropriate, heat-inducing daydreams about what the rest of his body might look like.

When Brett opened the car door for her in her driveway a few minutes later, she found herself wishing she were already inside. Not that there was anything wrong with Brett. On the contrary, he'd be a nice catch for some lucky woman. It just wasn't going to be her. And she dreaded what was going to be an awkward moment if he tried to kiss her good-night.

But he didn't move to walk her to the door. "I had a nice time tonight," he said.

"Me, too. Thank you."

There it was again, that little smile that said he knew something she didn't.

"What?"

He just shook his head. "After you get your other estimates, give me a call. I hope we can work together."

His shift back to talk of work surprised her. Despite his assertion otherwise, had she been that bad a date? If so, she really was losing her touch.

Brett glanced toward the house before he planted a quick kiss on her cheek. "Good night, Elissa."

"Good night." Elissa walked toward the front porch then looked back to wave as Brett drove away.

Instead of going inside, she sank onto the porch at the top of the steps. Her traitorous brain took her back to the night she'd sat here eating pie with Pete. That memory brought a smile to her face. It had been so simple, but it was the best night she'd had since before the storm. In all honesty, the best night she'd had in a long time.

As if her thoughts of Pete conjured him, he pulled into the driveway. Her heart rate kicked up a notch, even though she knew nothing could happen between them. They were friends, really good friends, and she knew herself. Despite the fact that she'd stopped her wandering ways when she'd moved in with Verona, she'd never really thought of herself as a settling-down type. She was content to go out with a guy once or twice, have a mutually good time and move on, no strings, no expectations. Pete deserved more than that, more than she could give him even if he was interested.

"Elissa?" Pete's gait slowed as he walked toward her. "Are you okay?"

He sounded so concerned that it hit her right in the middle of her heart. For a moment, she wondered what it was like, what India had with Liam, what Skyler had found with Logan. Was she so defective that she'd never allowed herself to think about finding that kind of deep and abiding love for herself? Or even something that lasted longer than a date or two?

"Elissa?" Pete said again as he drew close.

"I'm fine. Just enjoying sitting out here."

He stared at her for a moment before he sat beside her. "I'm surprised you're back so early."

"Yeah, me, too."

"You sure that guy didn't try something he shouldn't have?"

Elissa laughed a little. "Have you ever known me to not be able to take care of myself? And since when do I date complete jerks where that would even be necessary?"

Pete exhaled. "Point taken."

"You smell like horse. You been out for a ride?"

"Yeah."

Elissa detected a hint of frustration in his voice, which was odd because going for a ride had always been his way of relaxing, clearing his head. He certainly didn't seem overly relaxed at the moment.

Before she could ask him if something was wrong, he asked, "So, did you have a good time tonight?"

"It was fine. Brett's a nice enough guy. Even though the estimate he gave me for the rebuild about gave me a heart attack."

"Bad, huh?"

"Enough that I told him I should have had you shoot him."

Pete snorted. "You want to get the nursery open for business again, I'm thinking me shooting builders isn't a good idea."

Elissa gave a dramatic sigh. "And here I thought we were friends." She looked over in time to see an odd expression on Pete's face, one that felt as if he were interrogating her without uttering a word.

"What kind of friend would I be if I didn't give your dates a hard time?"

She bumped his shoulder with hers. "A good one, you dork."

He smiled at that, and the sight of it made her indescribably happy. Too many times, she'd seen him when he had nothing to smile about. And in that moment, she realized that it took very little effort from him to make her smile, too. Suddenly, she wanted nothing more than to spend more time with him. He didn't have to know anything about her inappropriate thoughts about him. And there wouldn't be anything odd at all about them hanging out since they'd been doing it for years, years in which she'd been blind to the man beyond the friend.

"You know what I was thinking about earlier?"

"No idea," he said.

"How India, Skyler and I used to go to the football games in high school to watch you guys play. We'd get a huge tub of popcorn and put so much butter on it that we probably used half the napkins the concession stand had on hand."

"What made you think of that?"

Thinking about you.

"I don't know. Just popped into my head." She paused, considering the wisdom of going on. "You working tomorrow night?"

"No, I'm working in the morning."

"Ah, your favorite shift. Well, since you've got the night off, I thought maybe we could all go to the game."

He glanced at her and gave her a crooked smile. "Eat a big tub of popcorn?"

"Of course."

He shook his head. "I don't know where you put it, woman."

"What, you're saying I eat too much?"

"I would never be that stupid."

She gave him a playful evil eye. "So you are smarter than the average man."

"I like to think so."

This felt good, teasing and laughing. But as Elissa glanced at Pete's profile, a new fear reached out and grabbed her. The fear that what she'd always shared with Pete was no longer enough.

Chapter Eight

"You've got to be kidding me," Greg Bozeman yelled at the ref who'd just made a call against the Blue Falls team that everyone on the home side of the field with eyes could see was wrong.

"Glad to see some things haven't changed," Pete said from where he sat next to Elissa.

"What, that the refs are still blind?" Greg asked.

"That you're still arguing with their calls."

Greg turned where he was sitting in front of them. "You tell me that wasn't a blown call."

"I didn't say you were wrong."

"The refs aren't the only thing that hasn't changed," Skyler said as she shifted her position. "These bleachers are still uncomfortable."

"They're better than the ones at the fairgrounds," Elissa said.

"Ugh, don't remind me. I'm not sure I can take bleachers two nights in a row."

"What, you're going to miss my triumphant return to the rodeo?" Pete laughed a little, probably because he was sitting with two actual rodeo cowboys.

Skyler patted his knee. "Sweetie, I'll come watch if

you promise not to fall off your horse and break your neck."

"Hey, I was pretty good."

"How long has it been since you were in a roping event?" Liam asked, a teasing look on his face.

"A while."

"Which means at least, what, five or six years?" Elissa only meant to add to the teasing, but she was suddenly worried about Pete getting hurt. After all, she'd seen both Liam and Logan get injured during rodeos, and they were professionals. Granted, team roping wasn't the same as riding a bucking bronc or a bull with a nasty attitude, but accidents still happened.

"I haven't been on a bike in ages, either, but I remember how to ride one." That drew several snickers.

"All I know is I'm bringing the thickest, fluffiest pillow I own to sit on." Skyler shifted in her seat again with a wince.

"The game's almost over," India said.

Elissa smiled at how good a time her friend seemed to be having. When they were in high school, India had been the most uncomfortable of their trio at games. Oddly enough, she did okay at school, was almost able to forget her horrible home life. But when they went to games, she had to be around adults who knew who her parents were, that they were the very epitome of useless. But India wasn't that insecure girl anymore. She'd made a good life for herself even before meeting Liam, but his love had made her blossom. Same with Skyler once Logan had convinced her he would never leave her as her father had repeatedly done to her mother.

"More popcorn?" Pete asked as he extended the tub toward her.

She waved it off. "No, I'm good."

"Did anyone get the memo that hell had frozen over?" Skyler asked.

"On second thought." Elissa stuck her hand in the popcorn bucket and pulled out a handful, which she promptly tossed at Skyler.

"Hey, no assaulting the pregnant lady," Skyler said as she put her hands up in defense.

"Weenie." Pete pitched a few more pieces of popcorn at Skyler, several of which went down the front of her shirt.

"Good aim, dude," Greg said, earning him a handful of popcorn courtesy of Skyler and Logan.

After several more volleys and a distinct clearing of the throat by the older woman a couple of bleachers behind them, they all managed to get control of themselves. Elissa wasn't the only one who was having trouble not laughing at them being scolded.

"Like I said, some things never change," Greg said.

After the game was over, they all headed for the parking lot.

"This was a good idea," India said. "We should do this again, a group outing."

"Only next time I need a date," Greg said. "This solo stuff is ruining my reputation. I'm what, the seventh wheel here."

Elissa looked at Pete in the same moment that he looked at her, but they quickly shifted their gazes away from each other. Neither of them said anything to draw attention to the fact that Greg was for some reason lumping them together as a couple. Thankfully, no one else seemed to notice.

"Man, I think there's still popcorn in my shirt," Skyler said.

Elissa was laughing when she stepped out from between two cars just as someone came racing down the gravel drive. One moment she registered the headlights aimed at her, and in the next someone grabbed her and shoved her out of the way. He'd already let her go before she realized it was Pete and that he was approaching the driver's side of the now-stopped car.

He pointed at the driver. "You need to slow down. It's a parking lot, not the interstate."

The guy yelled an obscenity at him. In the next moment, Pete reached through the driver's open window and grabbed the front of his shirt. "You're obviously not from here, so you don't know that I can arrest you and toss you in jail for reckless endangerment."

"Sorry, man." The driver looked through his windshield at Elissa. "Sorry."

She nodded then shifted her attention back to Pete. "It's okay. No harm done."

Pete slowly let go of the driver's shirt. "Don't go even one mile per hour over the speed limit on the way home."

The guy nodded before he much more slowly continued on his way.

Greg laughed. "Whoa, who knew Pete had some badass in him?"

Pete ignored him, instead watching the driver leave the parking lot. Then he glanced at Elissa. "You okay?"

"Yeah, fine." Except she suspected that the frantic beating of her heart had more to do with how incredibly attractive she found Pete at the moment than almost being run over. It was all she could do not to lick her lips as she took in the entirety of him—the familiar hat and boots, jeans and a blue T-shirt that covered that chest she couldn't purge from her thoughts. But it was the way the muscles in his forearms stretched taut, the way his hands were clenched into fists that made her uncharacteristically breathless. Who knew she had a weakness for a guy being all alpha protector?

They'd all resumed walking toward their cars when Skyler grabbed Elissa's arm and held her back, letting Pete get a little ahead. "Um, is there something we should know?"

Elissa managed to suppress her moment of panic as she met Skyler's gaze. "About?"

"What just happened. Pete going all knight in shining armor."

Elissa looked from Skyler to India and back. "In case you haven't noticed, he's a cop. Protecting the public is his job."

"I've never known Pete to accost a driver before," Skyler said.

"It could have been a little kid who ran out in front of him. Jerk was probably just pissed that his team lost, and he needed that attitude adjustment."

Elissa wasn't sure her friends were convinced, but there was nothing else she could say or do without making it obvious that she was trying too hard to deny anything between her and Pete. Plus, she wasn't lying. There wasn't anything between them, nothing that hadn't been there for years anyway.

"I'll catch you all later. I gotta get some sleep. The insurance agent is coming by tomorrow morning, hopefully with a big fat check."

"Good," India said. "About time."

Elissa followed Pete to her SUV, leaving the others

to wander off in different directions toward their own vehicles.

"What were Skyler and India all secretive about?"

Elissa deliberately didn't look at him as she slid into her side of the car. "Nothing."

She started the engine and headed out of the parking lot. They were halfway back to her house before the rapid-fire beating of her heart started to calm. She glanced over at Pete and noticed that he still seemed tense.

"Thanks for keeping me from becoming a pancake back there."

"No problem." But by the way he held himself, something was still bothering him.

"Are you okay?"

"I nearly punched that guy."

"I saw."

"I don't normally lose my temper like that."

Something shifted inside Elissa's chest, a sliver of... Was that hope that the reason Pete was so upset was because it had been her specifically who'd almost been hit?

She returned her attention to the road, scolding herself for continuing to allow those types of thoughts to find a home in her mind.

"Well, I think he had it coming." She laughed a little, trying to make light of the incident. She let a few moments pass by before she felt the need to fill the silence. "So, you and Charlie are really ready?"

"We practiced some today. We're rusty, but we're not exactly shooting for winning. Just filling in a slot."

She almost told him to be careful, but she held her tongue. It wasn't as if he was careless.

"I better not injure myself too badly, or Connor will kill me."

"Connor? Why, because he'd have to take extra shifts?"

"No, because I've got a date with his cousin Leah afterward."

That news hit Elissa harder than it should have, and her hands involuntarily tightened on the steering wheel until she forced herself to relax her grip.

"Oh, yeah. I guess a guy with a broken neck or cracked skull wouldn't be the best date in the world."

"Pretty sure I won't be that even if I stay intact."

"Why would you say that?" She winced at the tone of her voice, as if she might throw punches at anyone who suggested he wasn't a great date. "I mean, that's a bit defeatist, don't you think? Not the right attitude to take into a date."

"I'm just doing it as a favor to Connor so he can go out with Kristi McKee instead of feeling obligated to spend the evening with Leah."

That made her feel better. Not a lot, but enough that she didn't want to throttle this Leah person on sight. What was wrong with her? She should be wishing Pete well. He deserved to have a good time, to find someone special. Maybe it wasn't Leah, but who was to say?

The mere thought made her jaws tighten.

When they reached the house, she used the excuse of having to meet the insurance agent in the morning to head to bed. In reality, she just needed to be alone, without Pete within sight or her friends growing a little too suspicious. Sometime between now and when she emerged from her room in the morning, she had to find a way to forget these new, problematic feelings about Pete.

Because if she didn't, she didn't know how much longer she was going to be able to hide them.

As she sank down on the side of her bed, she sifted through her stack of mail she'd grabbed from the kitchen table. On the bottom was a large envelope from her mother, sent from Portugal. Inside she found a pair of green-and-gold teardrop earrings, a copy of a travel magazine with her mother's latest article in it and a letter. She opened it and started to read.

> Elissa, sweetie, I hope you're doing well and that repairs on the nursery are already under way. I feel so awful that I couldn't be there to hold you and make sure you were really okay after the tornado.

They'd talked only briefly the next day just before her parents were boarding a plane for China and a float down some river that was so remote Elissa wasn't even sure it had a name. Evidently, they'd made it back to civilization alive. She read the rest of the letter, which recounted some of their most recent adventures, including how her father was evidently now an honorary chieftain of a tribe in some hidden-away nook in Zimbabwe. Elissa laughed at the picture her mom had included of her dad in some sort of wild ceremonial headdress that had to weigh a ton.

Elissa lay on her side and opened the magazine to her mom's article. Her mom really did have a remarkable talent for making places come alive with her words, so much so that by the end of the article Elissa was ready to book a flight to the remotest corner of Africa.

Maybe that was what she needed, to get away, really away for a while. Someplace she didn't have to watch Pete go out with other women while she scolded herself for caring. Only she didn't have that luxury right now, not when her business lay in shambles. Her bank account wasn't the only one suffering from the absence of income. She needed to get back up and running as soon as she could, for the sake of her employees as much as herself, more even. Some of them had spouses and children depending on them. She had no one.

That one, inescapable thought weighed heavier with each passing moment as she changed into her pajamas and slid into bed. As she closed her eyes and begged for sleep to claim her, she couldn't help fantasizing about having the freedom to run away to some exotic locale where she had no worries, no responsibilities, no need to watch her every word and every movement when she was around Pete.

As she drifted closer to sleep, her mental travels changed. Suddenly, she wasn't alone. Someone stepped up beside her and entwined his fingers with hers. When she looked over at him, a smile spread across her face. And Pete smiled back.

"HEY, HON," VERONA said the next morning when Elissa entered the kitchen to fill her thermal mug with coffee. "How was the game last night?"

"Fun. Looks like they have a good team this year."

"That's good. Listen, I know you're in a hurry to get to work, but I wanted to run an idea by you."

"Okay." If this was more of her matchmaking, Elissa was going to scream.

"I thought we might throw Pete a surprise birthday party. With this the first year since his mom's been gone, I thought it might be good to surround him with friends.

And we can use it as an excuse to get him some things he lost in the storm."

Elissa searched her aunt's face for any hint of ulterior motive, but either it wasn't there or Verona was getting better at hiding it. "That's actually not a bad idea."

"You sound surprised."

"Well, I just never know what you have up your sleeve."

"Arms, dear, nothing more."

Yeah, as if she would ever believe that. Still, the party was an idea she could get behind. "I'll find out from Simon if Pete works that day, and if so what time he's on the schedule."

"Good. I'll take care of all the other details. You don't need anything else on your plate right now."

No, she didn't. If only she could carve out the large chunk of her brain being occupied by thoughts of Pete, about how he would no doubt have his arms around Leah at the music hall tonight.

"Something wrong?"

Elissa refocused on Verona. "No, why?"

"You just looked like you smelled something bad."

Elissa shook her head. "Just wishing I had a genie in a bottle who would grant me three wishes. One, a big fat insurance check. Two, being able to snap my fingers and have the nursery repaired and back open for business."

"And three?"

Satisfying her curiosity about what it felt like to kiss Pete without having to fear that it would ruin their friendship.

But she didn't say that. She shrugged. "Being able to eat anything I want without ever gaining an ounce."

Verona rolled her eyes and turned back toward the

toaster that had just ejected her bagel. "See you at the rodeo tonight."

Elissa was next to useless at work once she arrived. Even without the building being repaired, there was still plenty to do. However, concentration proved impossible as she kept checking the parking lot for Andy Freeman, her insurance agent. Once she got that insurance check in the bank, she could get the major work under way. After getting two more estimates on the repairs, she'd discovered Brett was right. His bid was going to be the winner. She doubted she'd even reach the bank before she called him. The sooner she got the existing building back up and running, the sooner she could begin the additions. Maybe then her life would settle back into some semblance of normal.

Well, except for where Pete was concerned. She doubted getting her business back on track was going to make her crazy attraction go away. If only it would.

"Elissa?"

She jerked her attention toward the door. "Oh, hey, Andy. I've been watching for you all morning, and then you sneak up on me."

He smiled, and she saw a hint of the mischievous boy who had loved to prank their teachers in high school. Never in a million years would she have imagined him growing up to be an insurance agent of all things. "Sorry about that." He extended an envelope to her. "I'm guessing this is what you were waiting for."

Elissa accepted the envelope and kissed Andy on the cheek. "You are officially my favorite person of the day."

"Oh, good. Can't say I hold that title with most people."

"I bet Stephanie proclaims you her favorite person every morning."

Stephanie Falconer had harbored the biggest crush on Andy all through high school, and he'd barely known she existed. It hadn't been until he'd accidentally rear-ended her car while she was sitting at a stoplight in San Antonio that he'd really noticed her. Six months and a little help from one Verona Charles later, and Stephanie Falconer had become Stephanie Freeman. A year after that, Stephanie had given birth to quite possibly the cutest set of twins to ever be born.

"She hasn't booted me out yet, so I guess I'm doing something right," he said.

"You two are so cute together." Elissa opened the envelope and pulled out the check. When she saw the amount, she stared at it for a long moment before turning the check to face Andy. "Is this a partial payment?"

"No, that's the full amount."

Elissa shook her head. "That can't be right. This isn't enough to do the repairs."

Andy gave her an apologetic look. "You had a policy for actual market value, not replacement cost." She must have looked confused. "The actual market value policy is less expensive, but since this building is several decades old it's depreciated quite a bit."

He said a few other things that went in one ear and out the other. The bottom line was that all her plans had just had a giant hole blasted right through the middle of them.

"I'm sorry, Elissa. I truly am."

"It's not your fault, Andy." No, it was hers for not understanding her policy. What the hell was she going to do?

After Andy left, she didn't even have time to try to think of a solution. She had plants to load and a booth to set up at the fairgrounds, a rodeo to get through. With the overwhelming need to bring in cash riding heavy on her, she added some clay pots, wind chimes and a couple of small birdbaths to her inventory. Maybe she'd get lucky and sell it all tonight. Since she'd been directly affected by the tornado, she fell into the category of booth runners who only had to donate a portion of tonight's proceeds.

Somehow she managed to get through the afternoon of setting up her booth and helping a couple of her neighbors get theirs ready before the gates opened. She had to keep busy or she feared she might fall apart. One more thing just might do her in. And she hated feeling this way, hated that fate had decided to dump load after load of crap on her. Was this payback for having a relatively carefree life until now? If so, she was pretty sure she would much rather have had it spread out a bit.

She looked up from taking a drink of water to see Pete leading a gray horse out of the back of Charlie's two-horse trailer. It must be the horse he was going to use to compete. She watched as he rubbed his hand along the animal's neck. Her breath caught when she imagined that same hand grazing her skin. Though she knew her thoughts were going down a scary road, she couldn't look away from how Pete moved, how good he was with the horse. It wasn't until he and Charlie led the horses out of sight that she was able to pull her gaze away.

With her booth prepped, she was left with nothing to do but think. And she just couldn't allow herself to think too much right now. After she got through tonight would be soon enough to figure out how she was going to lift her business up out of ruin, and stop lusting after her friend.

Unable to sit still, she walked down the lane between the various booths. There was everything from old tools and handmade quilts to a caricature artist and

Ryan Teague's carved wooden angels. She almost passed the booth next to Ryan's, but then a photo album caught her eye. She stepped closer to examine the cover of the album, which had been decoupaged with articles from the *Blue Falls Gazette,* including one about the high school football team's regional championship when she'd been in high school.

Though the conversation with Verona about throwing Pete a birthday party now seemed to have taken place ages ago instead of hours, she suddenly got the perfect idea for his present. "How much for the album?"

"Twenty dollars," the woman said.

Sure, she might not be in the best financial position right now, but she could afford twenty bucks for a friend who'd lost so much more than she had. One who was somehow meaning more to her every day by doing nothing more than sharing pie with her under a starry sky or keeping her from being mowed down by a ticked-off football fan armed with a couple thousand pounds of car.

Elissa bought the album and then a candy apple because, quite frankly, she was feeling sorry for herself. It wasn't pretty, but hey, sometimes life wasn't pretty.

The gates would be opening soon, so she started back toward her booth by walking up the next aisle over. She was impressed by how many people had decided to contribute their time and wares to the cause. If nothing else made her feel good today, that giving spirit did.

She was almost back to her booth when she noticed a display of handcrafted jewelry. An orange-and-turquoise necklace shaped like a flower caught her attention and she moved closer to run her fingers over the beadwork.

"The orange earrings come with it."

Elissa looked up to see a petite blonde walking toward

her from the front of the car parked behind the display. "It's beautiful work."

"Thanks. I enjoy it."

"Do you sell your stuff in shops?"

"Some, and I have an online store."

"I have a friend here in town who has a boutique. If you have anything that might be vintage-inspired, I bet she'd like to carry it."

"That sounds great."

"She'll be here tonight. I'll send her over."

"Thanks." The blonde glanced at their surroundings. "Do you have a booth?"

"Oh, yeah, sorry." Elissa extended her hand. "Elissa Mason. I own a nursery, so I've got the plants and yard décor up there." She pointed toward her booth, now manned by Verona.

"Great. I'll try to pop by later." The woman picked up one of her business cards from its holder at the end of the table and handed it to Elissa.

As soon as she saw the name, Elissa wondered what she had done to tick off fate so much. The words on the card seemed to taunt her.

Leah Murphy Custom Jewelry, with her name written in a fancy, flowing script. Somehow Elissa found the strength to meet the other woman's gaze. "You're Connor's cousin."

Leah smiled. "Yeah."

Connor Murphy's cousin.

Pete's date.

Hello, final straw.

Chapter Nine

Pete walked away from the arena after his and Charlie's ride, glad to be in one piece.

"At least we didn't come in dead last," Charlie said as he walked beside Pete.

"Glad I got a day job, though."

"You and me both, buddy." Charlie glanced back at the arena, where the bull riders were getting ready for their turns in the spotlight. "Must be like all that Spanish I learned in high school, use it or lose it."

Pete snorted. "Come on, let's get a drink and watch these crazy fools."

The honest truth was he needed a beer to relax. He was nervous about his date with Leah, and he had a distinct suspicion it had nothing to do with Leah at all. Well, other than he was going to feel guilty taking her out when he couldn't get his mind off the dream he'd awakened from that morning. The one that had him nearly bolting from the house before he could possibly run into Elissa and not be able to explain why he couldn't look her in the eye.

While he slid onto the end of the bleachers and tried focusing on the bull riders, his traitorous brain kept replaying how very real that dream had felt. The softness of Elissa's skin, the way she'd smelled like the flowers she was around all day, the warmth of her lips as he'd captured them with his own. And then… He couldn't think about what had come next or he was going to get very uncomfortable really quickly.

He thought back through everything that had happened since the night of the tornado, and he couldn't point to any one thing that had shifted his thinking about Elissa. It was almost as if it had always been there, and living under the same roof had simply flipped the "on" switch. Was that possible? Had that long-ago crush not really disappeared but simply gone into a long hibernation?

It didn't matter where it had come from or when. It was there now. What had once passed between them without a second thought now camped out in the front of his brain, playing over like a video clip on constant repeat. The pie on the front porch, dancing with her at the music hall, that night they'd fallen asleep together on the couch.

Pete only halfway watched the riders competing in the arena. All he wanted was to get the rodeo over with so he could get his obligation to Connor fulfilled, too.

And then do what? It wasn't as if he was going to tell Elissa one iota of what was going on in his head. He'd likely freak her out so bad she'd fly off to whatever remote corner of the world her parents were currently exploring just to get away from him.

No, if he were smart he'd focus on Leah and having a good time with her. She'd seemed nice enough when she'd stopped by the sheriff's office earlier and Connor had introduced them.

After the bull riding was over, Pete stood and took a fortifying breath. Calling himself an idiot for dreading a date with a pretty woman, he headed toward the market booths to find Leah's. As luck would have it, he came upon Elissa's first and saw her trying to wrestle a big pot into the back of her SUV.

"Here, let me help with that," he said as he stooped beside her and gripped the bottom and top edge of the pot, planter, whatever she called these big things people filled with flowers.

"I can get it."

"Yes, I can see that." He smiled at her, but it only earned him a snarl in response. "What's with you?"

"Nothing."

"And my name's Scooby-Doo."

"Hush and lift, Scooby."

Something was definitely bothering her, but he didn't miss the fact that she wasn't in the mood to talk about it. And when his dream from that morning picked that moment to pop into his head again, he made his escape.

When he found Leah, she was putting the last of her boxes in the back of her car.

"Oh, hey there," she said when she saw him. The big smile on her face made him feel good and guilty at the same time. "I heard you made it through your ride."

"Yeah, but I don't think I'll be taking the rodeo circuit by storm any time soon."

She lifted a bamboo wind chime that he recognized.

"You do some shopping, too?"

"Yeah, met a nice gal who runs the local nursery. Elissa, you probably know her. Bet you know everyone in a town this small."

"Close to it." He didn't feel like mentioning that not only did he know Elissa, but he was also bunking at her house and having really hot sex dreams about her that made him want to take an ice bath.

"Listen, I appreciate you being willing to hang out

with me tonight while Connor is off making his moves, but you don't have to."

Part of him wanted to take her up on the easy out, but a bigger part knew he'd feel like a giant heel if he did. "Nah, we're going to have a good time. Have you ever been to our music hall?"

"Once, a few years back. It still the most happening place in town?"

He smiled. "Yeah, but there's not much competition."

She laughed. "I don't know. I hear if you sit at the Frothy Stein long enough, you'll see either a fight or someone nearly lose an eye in a darts game."

Okay, so tonight wasn't going to be a chore after all. Leah was funny on top of being pretty. Maybe she was just what he needed to rid himself of thoughts that were going to get him into a heap of "can't explain myself" if he wasn't careful.

A few minutes later, they parked next to each other at the Blue Falls Music Hall. He offered her his arm and escorted her into the crowded building. "Would you like something to drink?"

"Not now. I think I feel like dancing. Come on." Leah grabbed his hand, and the next thing he knew he was on the dance floor. And Leah kept him there for several songs.

Even though he was having a good time, he found himself searching the crowd for Elissa. After he and Leah had been dancing for a while, he spotted Elissa at the bar with Greg Bozeman. A shot of stupid jealousy shot through him, and he refocused his attention on Leah. But after a couple of minutes, his gaze wandered in Elissa's direction again. Now she was talking to India, Skyler and Keri Teague. When India caught him looking their way, she had a serious look on her face. Was something wrong?

He resisted the urge to go check. He could talk to Elissa later, maybe tomorrow.

Try as he might, he couldn't keep his attention from slipping back toward the group of women. Only Elissa wasn't with them now. He scanned the crowd and noticed her talking and laughing with some cowboy he didn't recognize. If he'd thought that crazy stab of jealousy he'd experienced when he saw her laughing with Greg was strong, it was nothing compared to what slammed into him now. Thankfully he still had enough sense to know that he shouldn't give in to the irrational urge to go punch the guy.

He refocused on Leah and some story she was telling about when she and Connor were kids, something about him getting pushed out of a tree house that was the domain of the female cousins.

"He broke his arm. I felt bad, but he could have avoided the whole thing if he'd just read the sign. It clearly said No Stinky Boys Allowed."

He made himself smile and laugh at all the appropriate spots in her story, but it was hard to concentrate when his interest lay elsewhere. Despite trying not to, his gaze wandered back toward Elissa. Only she was gone again, and not with the cowboy she'd been talking to since he was leading another woman onto the dance floor.

He caught sight of Elissa heading toward the exit. For some reason, he got the impression that she had never been more tired.

"You like her, don't you?"

Pete shifted his attention back to Leah. "Excuse me?"

"Elissa. You like her." It wasn't a question this time, and oddly she didn't look upset. Instead, she was smiling.

"No, we're just friends."

"Liar." Leah laughed. "Don't look so shocked. Anyone with half a brain should be able to see how you can't keep your eyes off her."

"It's not like that."

"But you want it to be."

"Listen, Leah—"

She held up her hand. "Don't you dare apologize. There's no need."

He stopped dancing and stared at her. "Do you mean that, or am I going to regret it if I don't go ahead and apologize?"

Leah gripped his upper arms. "You'll only regret it if you don't tell her how you feel."

He narrowed his eyes at her. "Have you been talking to her aunt?"

"Who?"

He shook his head. "Never mind. I'm sorry I was such a crappy date. Don't tell Connor, okay?"

"If you'll introduce me to the hottie at the bar, it's a deal."

He glanced toward the bar and knew instantly that she had to mean Greg. That dude was a serious chick magnet without even trying overly hard.

After introducing Leah to Greg and sending them off to the dance floor, he turned to find India close to him.

"Hey, India."

"Pete." Uh-oh, something was not right with the way she said his name.

"Is Elissa okay?"

"You should ask her that."

He opened his mouth to ask what she meant but then thought better of it, especially when he saw Verona approaching. Instead, he let someone pushing past him to get to the bar give him the excuse to turn away and head for the door.

Even after he got outside and was able to take a deep breath, the world still felt as if it had tilted a little off its axis. If he were smart, he'd go back inside and find someone to dance with, or maybe drown his thoughts about Elissa. But he didn't. Rather, he found himself walking to his truck and driving the short distance back to the house.

When he pulled into the driveway, his headlights revealed that Elissa's half of the garage sat empty. He knew her well enough to know where she would go if she was upset. It didn't happen often, but whenever she'd been angry or sad in the past, she'd buried herself in work at the nursery. She'd once said that surrounding herself with plants and inhaling the earthy scent of potting soil calmed her.

He backed out of the driveway and drove the three miles to the nursery. He expected to see more lights on than the ones that always burned for security purposes. At first he thought maybe he'd been wrong, until he saw her SUV parked in the lot.

He parked next to her and slid out of his truck. When he tried the side door, it was locked. The front door was in the part of the building that was damaged and currently blocked off by temporary fencing to keep out animals and anyone who got the idea to loot the place.

"Elissa?"

He got no response, which set his nerves to buzzing. He was about to call out more loudly when he heard a shuffling sound in the dark.

"I'm over here."

It was Elissa's voice, but it didn't sound right.

Pete saw her then, sitting on a bench cloaked in darkness. "Are you okay?"

She didn't immediately answer, which only served to make him more anxious. Then he heard her sniff. She was crying, and he wanted to do incredible violence to whomever or whatever had made her cry.

"No," she said. "I'm not."

Those words broke his heart more than seeing his home wiped from the face of the earth.

ELISSA HAD LOST track of how long she'd been sitting and staring at the rubble that was the front of her nursery, feeling helpless and alone and confused. When she'd realized that being here wasn't giving her the comfort she sought, that was when she'd lost the battle with her tears.

Pete kneeled in front of her. "Elissa, what's wrong? Are you hurt?"

She wanted so badly to lift her hand and rest it against his cheek, but she slid it under her leg instead before she could embarrass herself further. "Not physically."

His stance stiffened. She couldn't see it, but something about the air around him told her his muscles had tightened the same way they had when he'd confronted the driver who'd almost plowed into her.

"Did that guy at the music hall say something to you?" Pete sounded as if all she would have to say was yes and he'd make the guy wish he'd never set foot in Texas.

She shook her head. "No, this has nothing to do with that." Well, not entirely. But she wasn't about to tell him that as she'd been flirting with the cowboy, all she could think about was Pete dancing with Leah, of how she wanted to be held in his arms instead. If she confessed that, there was no going back. She'd destroy her relationship with him, and she didn't think she could handle that right now. Or ever.

He glanced over his shoulder. "Is it the nursery? You'll be back open before you know it."

She swiped at a tear, angry that she'd let herself be reduced to crying in the dark. Elissa Mason was the life of the party, always happy, always up for a joke and a good time.

But that was before her life had started falling down about her ears.

"The insurance check…it wasn't enough."

"What?"

"It's not enough to make the repairs, let alone replace all the shattered stock. I'll have to use the loan I got to expand to fill in the difference. And who knows if business will ever be what it was, let alone increase?"

Pete shifted onto the bench beside her and wrapped his strong arm around her shoulders. "I'm so sorry, Lis."

She smiled a little at that. It felt good, intimate when he called her that, the only person to do so. She allowed herself the comfort of laying her head on his shoulder. "I know I don't have the right to complain. After all, I'll be able to rebuild and open again. And so many others, you included, have lost so much more."

Pete squeezed her tighter to him. "Stop doing that."

"What?"

"Making it sound as if you don't have the right to mourn your loss."

"But you lost your home, everything. Others lost their lives."

"And you lost something that is dear to your heart,

not to mention the plans for expanding. Those are no small things."

"But—"

"No buts."

She choked on the giant lump that formed in her throat and the fresh tears that streamed down her cheeks. Unable to hold it in any longer, she released the reins on her pain and really cried. Pete pulled her even closer, wrapping both arms around her. With her cheek pressed against his chest, she circled his waist with her arms, as well.

Pete rubbed his hand up and down her arm, and that only made her cry all the harder because a part of her wanted this moment to be happening because of more than friendship. She became intensely aware of the feel of his chest beneath her cheek, the cut of his muscles where her hands lay against his back. It took an incredible amount of self-restraint for her to not let her hands slide up his back, exploring the contours that were totally unknown to her.

When Pete kissed the top of her head, she froze before gradually pulling away from him. Their gazes connected, and a burning need flamed to life within her, the need to take a chance with him. But she couldn't, not when she'd be forced to still see him even if he spurned her. Blue Falls wasn't a big enough town where you could avoid someone for very long.

Pete used his thumb to wipe at the wetness on her cheek. "I hate to see you cry."

"You've never seen me cry. I'm not a crier, current state to the contrary."

"That's why I hate it. You're supposed to be happy."

She sighed and looked away. "Even happy people have

their hearts broken sometimes." As the words left her lips, they felt as if they were aimed more at her longing for him than the damage to her business. She should really pull away from his touch, stand to put some distance between them. But she couldn't, not even when she feared his continued nearness might lead her to do something she'd live to regret.

Pete touched her chin and gently turned her face toward him. "Is there anything I can do?"

Elissa's lips parted as she stared up into his eyes. "I…" A voice inside her mind told her to go for it, but she somehow scraped together enough self-control to keep from leaning toward him.

But then Pete's gaze dropped to her lips for a heart-stopping moment before it met and held hers again. He moved his thumb ever so slightly to graze her bottom lip. Her breathing stuttered at the feel of his touch. Pete leaned toward her so slowly that at first she didn't notice he was moving. When he was close enough that she felt his warm breath against her mouth, her heart remembered to beat again and made up for lost time by launching into a galloping frenzy.

Pete's lips touched hers tentatively at first, so much so that she feared she was imagining the entire encounter. Afraid he would pull away, she leaned toward him. Her movement seemed to ignite Pete because in the next moment he slid his hand along her jaw to the back of her head and really kissed her. His mouth was warm, firm and soft at the same time as his lips moved against hers. Unable to stop herself, she moaned and slid closer to him. Her head spun with how good it felt to taste him. She wanted more, much more, but the ringing of a phone caused him to pull away abruptly. It took Elissa a few heartbeats to realize it was his phone and that he was standing while he answered it.

She licked her lips, tasting him all over again, as she tried to calm her racing heart. What had they done?

They hadn't just stepped past the point of no return. They'd leapt across it and left it far behind them. Unable to sit still, she got to her feet and took a few steps in the opposite direction.

Pete ended the call and turned toward her. In the darkness, she couldn't read the expression on his face.

"I've got to go. Seems there's an all-out brawl going down at the Stein, and Simon and Connor need backup."

"Okay."

Instead of leaving, however, he closed the distance between them. "Are you okay?"

She knew he wasn't talking about the nursery or the insurance check this time. She forced a smile, hoping that what had just happened didn't ruin everything between them, a friendship more than a decade in the making. "Yeah, fine."

He reached out and ran his thumb across her cheek again even though it was dry now. "I'll see you later?"

She nodded, unable to speak for fear of crying again. Only this time, the tears that threatened were because of the gentleness he showed her.

He lingered a moment longer and then hurried toward his truck.

After the sound of his engine disappeared into the distance, she sank back onto the bench and replayed the kiss in her mind. She ran her fingertips across her lips, hardly able to believe that she'd just kissed one of her best friends. And that it had been incredible, just as she'd imagined it would be. Elissa couldn't help wondering at how deeply he might have kissed her, how he might have held her if mayhem hadn't broken out among the drunkards at the Frothy Stein.

But the longer she sat, the more she started to worry that despite how much she'd enjoyed the kiss she might have made a horrible mistake. It was one thing to kiss Pete in the dark when she was upset and he was trying to comfort her, but would it be uncomfortable between them in the light of day, with other people around? Had her weakness just ensured that she and Pete would grow apart?

Elissa leaned forward, elbows on her knees, and dropped her face into her hands. She shook her head, trying to clear the worry. Because she'd rather have gone her entire life not knowing what it was like to kiss Pete than to lose his friendship.

She wondered if he was already regretting the kiss. When she saw him again, if he acted as if nothing had happened she would somehow find the strength to do the same. Even though she suspected it might kill her inside. But she'd rather ensure the safety of their friendship than not have him at all.

MOST NIGHTS, THE FEW jail cells they had at the sheriff's department sat empty or only had a single occupant. Tonight they stood full, and another guy had been carted off by the state police because he had an outstanding warrant in Texarkana.

Pete walked out of the holding area to see Simon working his jaw where he'd been punched.

"I guess we earned our paychecks tonight," Simon said.

"You can say that again." Pete would rather have

stayed on that bench with Elissa than collecting his own shiner courtesy of a dude who had been more mountain than man.

"Hope you don't have any more dates coming up," Simon said as he indicated Pete's eye. "You're not going to be pretty in the morning."

The image of Elissa taking care of his injuries made his body heat all over. Even when he'd been dodging punches and slapping on cuffs earlier, he hadn't been able to wipe the feel and taste of Elissa from his mind. Or the worry that giving in to his sudden desire to kiss her had been a colossal mistake.

But she'd reciprocated. He kept telling himself that, and hoping that she wasn't having second thoughts.

"He's definitely not going out with my cousin again." Connor walked by and playfully punched Pete in the shoulder.

"I did exactly what she wanted."

"Yeah, introduced her to Greg."

"Greg's a good guy."

"Who has probably gone out with every woman in this county at least once."

"I think Leah can hold her own. After all, she pushed you out of her tree house. And from what I hear, you screamed all the way to the ground."

Connor faked another punch, this one to Pete's gut, before grabbing his keys and heading for the door. "I don't know about you two, but I plan to enjoy the rest of my night off."

When Pete glanced at Simon, his boss nodded toward the door. "Go on. I'll watch these losers."

But when Pete reached his truck, he sat inside staring down the largely deserted stretch of Main Street. He couldn't decide if having the kiss interrupted earlier was a good or bad thing. He definitely knew what his body thought, but what would have happened if he hadn't received the call to help bust up the fight? Would they have gone too far? Would Elissa have pushed him away? No way of knowing now.

Wanting to see her before too much time went by and he drove himself crazy overthinking things, he drove to the house and was glad to see her car in the garage. But when he stepped inside the house, she wasn't in any of the common areas. He paused outside her bedroom door.

"Elissa?" He said it low in the hope that Verona wouldn't hear him.

When he got no response, his heart sank. Granted, she might have fallen asleep, but he couldn't help wondering if she were awake on the other side of the door holding her breath until he walked away. With a sigh, he did just that.

Chapter Ten

The last thing Elissa wanted to do the next morning was go have breakfast with India and Skyler. Nothing against her friends, but they knew her too well. If they figured out something was off with her, she wasn't sure how she would explain it away. She had to admit a little part of her wanted to ask their advice. But another part wanted to keep what had happened between Pete and her to herself, at least until she figured out how he felt about it now that the moment was past. Of course, that would be easier to determine if she didn't keep avoiding him.

But she was pretty sure that facing him and having him either tell her their kiss was a mistake or pretend it hadn't happened was going to give her a punch to the chest she wasn't sure she could handle.

Knowing that avoiding her friends would cause even more scrutiny than willingly going through with her breakfast commitment, she took a deep breath and left her room.

"Good morning, hon," Verona said as Elissa entered the living room. "You off to breakfast with the girls?"

"Yeah."

"Well, don't sound so excited about it."

"I didn't sleep well last night." Not a lie.

"Pete must not have, either. I heard him up even earlier than me this morning." Verona set her knitting in her lap. "Speaking of Pete, do you think we should get him separate presents or go in on something bigger together? Lord knows the boy needs everything."

It took a moment for Elissa to realize Verona was talking about Pete's surprise birthday party. Damn, she had a lot to do between now and then. "I've got something already."

"Okay. Well, I've invited everyone and told them to be here no later than five-thirty and to park a street over. Since Pete gets off work at six, I'm going to call him shortly before that and feign some plumbing emergency to make sure he comes straight here."

"Sounds good." Before Verona could pull her further into conversation or pick up on some hint that Elissa was hiding something, she made for the door. "Considering how much Skyler hates mornings, I better not keep her waiting."

A few minutes later, Elissa pulled into the parking lot of the Wildflower Inn, which Skyler owned. Since she'd fallen head over heels in love with Logan Bradshaw, Skyler lived out at their ranch instead of in her apartment at the inn. A wave of loneliness hit Elissa as she thought about Skyler at the ranch with Logan, and India living her cozy life with Liam and Ginny in her little house complete with white picket fence. It still didn't seem possible that both of her friends were pregnant. She felt oddly left out, left behind.

Shaking off that bizarre train of thought, she headed inside to the inn's dining room.

"Our earliest riser is the last one here," Skyler said. "All is not right with the world."

She had no idea.

Elissa stuck her tongue out at her friend before heading for the buffet. At the scent of food, her stomach growled, reminding her that she hadn't eaten dinner the night before. And she'd been so upset at lunch that she'd barely touched her sandwich. Consequently, she was ravenous.

India shook her head when Elissa sat down. "Where do you put all that?"

"In my very empty stomach."

"Are you feeling okay? You left the music hall early last night."

"Had a long day." She took a bite of her scrambled eggs before noticing that India was still staring at her as if she knew something more was going on. She had to give her something she'd believe, so she offered up the truth.

"I can't stop thinking about the insurance and how much it's going to cost to rebuild." She didn't mention how she'd shared the same information with Pete the night before followed by a kiss for a chaser. A kiss she couldn't get out of her mind.

India gave her a sympathetic look. "At least you had the loan already. You can rebuild, make some improvements. Just not the expansion."

"I know I should be happy. I just…"

"Feel like you've taken a step back," Skyler said.

"Several." She shook her head. "I need to get my head on straight, though, and be thankful that I've fared as well as I have." Knowing something with your mind and feeling it in your heart were two different things, though.

They ate for a couple of minutes before Skyler sat back in her chair. "Well, I have some news."

"You've set a date to make an honest man out of Logan finally," Elissa said.

"Yes, this Saturday."

Elissa choked on her bacon. "Nothing like a little advance notice."

"We just decided last night. Since his family is coming for a visit and we want to keep it really simple, we thought we'd just go ahead and do it then at the ranch. Especially since we don't know if we'll get his family out of North Dakota again any time in the near future."

India squeezed Skyler's hand. "It sounds perfect."

They spent the next several minutes going over details.

"Seems like it's going to be a week of parties," India said as she looked at Elissa. "Is there anything you need for us to do for Pete's party?"

"Actually, yeah. I've been so busy that I haven't been able to finish getting his present put together. Since he lost all his pictures, I thought I'd ask around about copying any photos people have of him and his family, maybe some school pictures."

"That's a great idea," India said. "I'd think that would be the hardest part of losing your home, all the things you couldn't replace."

"Bet he's going to love the pictures of the party with that shiner he's sporting this morning," Skyler said.

Elissa paused with her glass halfway to her mouth. "What?"

"Didn't you hear about the fight at the Stein last night? They arrested half a dozen people."

"I heard about it, but I didn't know Pete got hurt."

Skyler made a circular motion around her eye. "Yeah, he got clocked by a guy who had to outweigh him by a hundred pounds."

Elissa's grip on her emotions about Pete evidently slipped because the moment her eyes met India's, she knew her friend had put Elissa's actions the night before together with her reaction to Pete's injury and come up with something besides friendship.

"Is something going on between you and Pete?"

Skyler jerked her attention up from her plate as if someone had just announced the pope was coming to Blue Falls.

Elissa opened her mouth to answer, but nothing came out.

"I saw you watching him last night when he was dancing with Connor's cousin." India wore an understanding expression.

Elissa set her fork on the edge of her plate, her appetite gone. "He kissed me."

"What?" Skyler's eyes grew so big it would be comical if Elissa weren't so dang confused.

"After I left the music hall, I went out to the nursery. I'd just had a horrible day, and I needed some time alone to try to figure out why I suddenly started feeling differently about Pete. I mean, it doesn't make a bit of sense, right?"

"Why not?" India leaned forward. "You've been good friends for a long time."

"Exactly. We're friends."

"Lots of couples start out as friends."

"We're not a couple. We're... I don't really know what we are now."

"And you're avoiding him. That's why you didn't know he was injured."

Elissa nodded. "I kept hoping it was just an infatuation and would go away. But it's not. If anything, it's growing stronger." She dropped her face into her hands for a moment before looking at her friends again. "What am I going to do? I don't want to ruin our friendship."

"After you kissed, how did he act?"

"That's when he got the call about the fight and had to leave. But he seemed fine." At least she hoped so.

"Then go with it, see what happens. You never know, true love could have been right under your nose the entire time."

"Or maybe I should just act as if nothing happened. I mean, he'll likely be leaving Blue Falls soon anyway. He applied to the state police academy again, and he doesn't have anything preventing him from going this time."

"Then you need to make your move before it's too late."

"I don't know." Elissa shifted her attention to Skyler, who'd been unusually silent on the topic. "What do you think?"

Skyler didn't answer immediately, which made Elissa's stomach clench.

"Skyler?"

"I want you to be happy, but I'm not sure this is the right thing to do."

"What?" India's surprise was evident in her tone.

"I'm not trying to be mean, but I'm afraid Pete will get hurt. He's a good guy and has lost too much already."

"Elissa would never hurt Pete. You know that."

Skyler glanced at India. "Not intentionally." She shifted her gaze back to Elissa. "But you like to flit from guy to guy, and there's nothing wrong with that when there's no danger of hurting someone. But think about how Pete is. He's a commitment kind of guy. If you're not ready to commit to him wholeheartedly, I don't think you should string him along."

Elissa didn't know whether to be sad or angry, but both emotions twisted up inside her. At the same time, she knew Skyler was right. When had she ever stuck with one guy for more than a couple of weeks? She couldn't even explain why she was the way she was, not when her parents had a loving marriage and she'd given up the traveling life for a more stable, settled one. Was it her way of still holding on to a little of the carefree existence she'd known the first fifteen years of her life? Had she just not found the right person to make her change her ways?

Could Pete be that person? Was it possible that India was right and true love had been right under her nose the entire time? Did she love Pete? Of course she did, but was it romantic love? She had no idea how she could distinguish between the love she'd always felt for her friend and what might be more than that.

"Don't listen to Skyler," India said. "Listen to your heart."

"No, she's right. Pete deserves to have someone special."

"You're special."

Elissa shoved her chair back. "I can't deal with this right now. I have too much else to deal with." She stood. "See you at the party."

She heard India call her name as she walked away, but she didn't stop or acknowledge it. She had to get out of the building before the echo of Skyler's words caused her to dissolve into tears.

PETE PAUSED HALFWAY down the corridor to Skyler's office at the Wildflower Inn. He didn't know why he was hesitant to ask about renting the apartment she'd vacated. After all, Elissa's avoidance of him for the past couple of days told him loud and clear that his kissing her had been the mistake he'd feared. Damn it, why had he listened to his desire instead of what little common sense he possessed?

He stared at the door that led to Skyler's former apartment. What better day than his birthday to gift himself with his own space again? He could come and go as he liked without worrying about Verona's matchmaking or making Elissa uncomfortable. Or torturing himself by being so near Elissa, knowing that he'd screwed everything up.

With renewed determination, he walked the rest of the way to Skyler's office and knocked on the open door.

Skyler looked up from her desk and seemed startled to see him. "Pete. What are you doing here?"

He hadn't considered that Elissa might have told India and Skyler about the kiss, but now he had to wonder. Deciding it didn't matter, he gestured behind him. "I was hoping I could rent your old apartment if it's not already spoken for."

"Oh. Well, no. Something wrong at Verona's?"

Hell, she definitely knew about the kiss. He clamped down on the need to ask her what Elissa had said. "No, but I've imposed enough."

Skyler looked as if she was holding back some questions of her own. "I've still got a lot of my stuff in there, so I'd need some time to get it out."

"That's no problem."

"It'll have to wait until after the weekend. Logan and I are getting married Saturday out at the ranch. We'd love for you to be there."

He smiled for what felt like the first time in days. "Congratulations." He was truly happy for her, same as he was when India and Liam tied the knot. But another part of him felt hollow, particularly today.

That empty feeling weighed him down all day during his shift. It might seem silly but he missed the fact that he wasn't going to have a birthday cake made by his mom. Even when she'd been ill that last year of her life, she'd rallied long enough to bake him a cake and write "I love you, Petey" on the top. She hadn't called him that since he was a little boy, and something about that moment, her slipping into the past in even the simplest way, had made him realize she wasn't going to win the fight this time. He was going to lose her, be left totally alone.

He didn't make a habit of feeling sorry for himself, but every once in a while it snuck up on him.

He was about to ask Connor if he wanted to hit the Stein tonight when his phone rang. When he checked the screen, his heart jumped a bit. But Elissa wouldn't be home this time of day. No, like every other day, she would work at the nursery until well after dark. He didn't even know what she could be doing out there so much, not until the building was repaired.

Pushing away questions he couldn't answer, he answered, "Hey, what's up?"

"Pete, hon. I was wondering if you might come straight home after your shift. I seem to have a plumbing issue I'm not quite strong enough to fix myself."

Everything else she said faded for a moment as he focused on the word *home* and how Verona's house wasn't his home at all. He didn't have one. No family, no home and likely no more friendship with Elissa.

He silently cursed himself and refocused on Verona's problem. "What's going on?"

"The pipe under the kitchen sink is leaking."

"You need me to come over there now?"

"No, no need. It'll wait a few more minutes. I've got a bucket under there."

"Okay, be there in a bit."

The last fifteen minutes of his shift crawled by. How sad was it that he was actually looking forward to playing plumber? That said a lot about the state of his life right now. Maybe he'd hear from the academy soon, and he could just start over somewhere else besides Blue Falls. Maybe that's what he needed, a clean break.

When he pulled into the driveway, he wasn't the least bit surprised to see Elissa wasn't home. He had to talk to her soon, find out from her own lips whether he was right in his assumption that she didn't want to get any more involved than that one kiss in the dark when she'd been upset and in need of comfort.

He stepped through the door from the garage expecting to see Verona in the kitchen. Instead, he jumped as a houseful of people yelled, "Surprise!"

He scanned the room as Logan popped a balloon and several people blew noisemakers that reminded him of New Year's Eve.

Verona stepped forward with a huge smile on her face. "Happy birthday, hon." She lifted up on her toes and kissed him on the cheek.

"You are one sneaky woman."

"I might have had a little help." She winked and nodded toward her left.

He glanced that way and saw Elissa leaning against the chair where Verona usually sat to do her knitting or to read. She gave him a small, tentative smile that lifted his hopes probably more than it should.

Over the next few minutes, he found himself talking to one well-wisher after another. And then Keri Teague brought out the cake. As soon as he looked at it, he laughed. It wasn't one of her usual beautiful creations. Well, he was sure the cake itself was good, but on the top she'd drawn a cartoon cop with a huge black eye. Underneath were the words her husband had spoken to Pete the night of the bar fight. "Duck next time."

Pete allowed Keri to serve him a huge piece of cake including the black eye portion of the icing before moving out of the way so others could get slices. He made his way over to stand next to Elissa.

"Skyler was right," she said. "You do have quite the shiner."

He lifted his slice of cake. "A fact I don't think I'm going to live down any time soon."

She smiled, a real smile this time, and the mere sight of it was the best gift he could have received. Maybe things would be okay between them after all.

"I'm sorry if what I did the other night was wrong," he said low so no one else could hear him.

Elissa glanced around the room. "It's fine."

Fine as in she didn't hold it against him, or fine as in she wouldn't mind it happening again? Damn, why were women so hard to read?

"Come on now, birthday boy," Verona said once everyone had their cake. "You've got presents to open."

"I suddenly feel five years old," Pete said to Elissa.

"Who knows, maybe there will be a toy train in your presents."

He smiled at her, glad that their friendship was still intact. He tried not to think about how he wouldn't mind there being more between them.

As he headed for the chair Verona indicated, he looked

at the faces surrounding him. "You all didn't have to do this."

"Yeah, we did," Simon said. "Or Verona was going to find new and interesting ways to make us wish we had."

Verona swatted Simon on the arm. "Hush, you."

After some laughter and a bit more teasing, Pete started opening presents. Dishes and a toaster oven were followed by a couple of gift cards from Grater's Shop-Mart. He had thought he was done when Elissa handed him a box covered in blue-striped paper.

"Thanks."

"You don't even know what it is yet."

"Well, unless there's a live lizard in here, I think I'm safe in my thanks."

As he met her gaze, he thought he saw anticipation there. Curious, he pulled the top off the box. Inside was a photo album covered in old newspaper clippings. His heart ached for a moment at the thought of all the pictures he'd lost. He no longer had a single photo of his parents, and he feared losing the memory of what they looked like.

He opened the album to see what clippings were on the inside cover, but his breath caught as soon as he saw what was inside. There on the first page was an eight-by-ten image of him with his parents when he was about seven. He was holding the trophy he'd won in Little League baseball. A lump forming in his throat, he flipped the pages to see copies of his school photos, candid shots taken at community events, several from his team-roping days, a picture a bunch of them had taken together during their senior prom. His eyes went right to Elissa, wearing that long gold dress with her dark hair piled up on top of her head. She'd looked every bit the beauty queen she'd been.

He realized in that moment that his new attraction toward her wasn't new at all. Somewhere deep down, that first crush he'd had on her when they were fifteen hadn't gone away. But he'd buried it so far down inside himself that he hadn't consciously realized an ember still existed. Being near her had simply blown enough air on it for it to flicker into a flame. And the kiss, well…enough with the fire analogies.

He paused halfway through the album when he came to a picture of the two of them sitting at her kitchen table putting together that Roman Coliseum diorama they'd had to make for history class. He smiled at the memory of her threatening to smack him upside the head if he didn't stop staging fights between their clay gladiators that usually ended in one or both losing a limb or even a head.

His heart swelling, Pete looked up and met Elissa's eyes. He knew how much work it must have taken for her to track down these photos to copy. That she'd done so while going through so much touched him so deeply that he suddenly wished they were alone.

"Thank you. This means a lot to me." So much more than anything money could buy.

"You're welcome."

Over the next several minutes, he got drawn into one conversation after another. If any of the people around him were paying attention, they would notice how often his gaze shifted to wherever Elissa was in the room. Though he appreciated everyone attending the party, he was glad when they began to leave.

India, Skyler and their other halves were the last to depart. There was something different in Skyler's eyes when she pulled back from giving him a hug, but he couldn't identify it. He didn't have a chance to ask, either, since India reached up to give him a kiss on the cheek before ushering Skyler out the door.

After closing the front door behind them, he turned to see Verona exit the kitchen.

She glanced over her shoulder to where Elissa was stuffing the last of the dirty paper plates in the trash. "I don't know about you two, but I'm beat," Verona said. "I'm calling it a night."

Pete crossed the room and pulled the older woman into his arms. "Thank you, for everything."

Verona patted his back. "You deserved it, sweetie." She stepped away. "Now I'm taking my old, creaking bones to bed."

As she headed down the hall, neither he nor Elissa moved until they heard Verona's door shut. When he finally looked at Elissa, she reminded him of a rabbit poised to bolt away.

"Thank you for the album," he said, feeling at a loss about how to start a conversation now that their kiss stood between them.

She smiled a little. "You said that already."

"I mean it. No one's ever gotten me anything that means more."

She met his gaze and thankfully didn't look away. "I knew it's what I'd want if I were in your situation."

A long, awkward moment stretched between them before they both started to speak at the same time.

"I better go to bed, too," she said.

As she moved to follow in Verona's footsteps, an unexpected but desperate need to keep her from leaving gripped Pete. "Wait."

She looked back at him, a questioning look in her eyes but nervousness tensing her body.

"Would you like to go for a walk?"

"I don't think that's a good idea."

He took a step toward her. "Why not?"

"You know why."

"Because we kissed."

Elissa looked nervously down the hall. "Yeah. I don't want you getting the wrong idea."

His chest tightened. "What wrong idea would that be?"

"That it was more than it was. I had a weak moment, nothing more."

He'd questioned enough people since becoming a cop to know when someone wasn't telling the truth. It was even easier with Elissa since he knew her so well. His heart leapt at the fact that right now Elissa was being less than truthful. "I don't believe you."

"Pete—"

He closed the rest of the distance between them. "Tell me you didn't like it. Tell me that truthfully and I'll never bring it up again."

When she opened her mouth to speak, a flood of uncertainty seized his body. Could he have been wrong? But she couldn't say the words, not without lying.

Pete lifted his hand to the side of Elissa's face, marveling at the softness of her skin. "You're not the only one who's been wondering if we made a mistake."

She looked up at him, a sliver of hurt in her eyes. "So you think it was?"

"I don't know. I hope not."

"Because we're friends?"

He nodded. "I don't know when it changed, but it did. I can't stop thinking about you."

He saw a fear in her eyes he'd never seen before. In that moment, he wanted nothing more than to erase that fear, to guarantee that there was no reason for her to feel it. But how could he do that when he wasn't sure himself?

Their history flashed through his mind, and it came to him. He'd treat her like always, just with some kissing thrown in. He smiled at the thought. "Since it's my birthday, you could just say that any kissing was part of my present."

She lifted an eyebrow at that, a reaction so like the normal Elissa that a bit of his anxiety faded. "That's a line if I've ever heard one."

He shrugged. "I'm a guy. What can I say?"

She grew serious again. "That if we give in to this, you promise it won't ruin what we already have. I can't stand the idea of losing you as a friend because we did something stupid."

Moving slowly, he took another step closer to her and ran his hand into her hair at the back of her head. His heart beating fast, he leaned toward her. "I promise," he said just before he captured her lips with his.

Chapter Eleven

Fear bolted through Elissa as Pete's lips met hers. They were no longer cloaked in darkness, and she couldn't hide behind the excuse of having had a horrible day full of upsetting news. They couldn't claim it was a onetime thing.

But as Pete wrapped his arm around her and pulled her close, deepening the kiss, all of that faded away, replaced by a rush of heat and yearning she'd never felt before. Without thinking about it, she circled his waist with her arms, running her hands up his back. Pete made a sound of appreciation that caused her to want even more. She opened her mouth, allowing him entry.

This shouldn't feel so good, not with Pete, but it did. Oh, how it did.

When he broke the kiss, Pete left her breathless. His smile was full of mischief, as if he knew exactly how his mouth had scrambled her brains.

"Not bad for a birthday kiss," he said.

He wanted to tease, did he? Well, two could play that game. She shrugged. "It was okay."

She saw the challenge in his eyes a moment before he pulled her to him again and stole her breath and ability to think coherently with a kiss so thorough her knees actually weakened. She'd always thought that was a cliché in novels because she'd kissed a lot of guys and never come close to feeling as unsteady as she did in this moment.

How had she not realized what she'd been missing all these years?

Because Pete wasn't a loud, showy guy wearing his testosterone on his sleeve. Not that he wasn't 100 percent red-blooded male, because he obviously was, but he'd always been just Pete, her dear friend, the guy next door. Not once had she imagined him naked in her bed, but she sure was imagining that now as he pressed his body close to hers. It was obvious what their kissing was doing to him, and the feel of his arousal pressed against her stomach along with the memory of seeing his bare chest had her body buzzing, as well.

Just as she was considering pushing him down on the couch and having her way with him, he abruptly pulled away. With a wicked smile, he headed down the hall. "See you tomorrow. Sweet dreams."

Stunned by his sudden departure and trying to remember how to breathe normally, she tried to gather enough brain cells together to realize what he'd done. He shot her another mischievous smile before he slipped into his room and closed the door behind him.

Oh, he'd just declared war. And she was very imaginative when it came to paybacks.

When an image of tying him to his bed and teasing him unmercifully with her tongue entered her head, her legs wobbled enough that she sank onto the arm of the couch before she fell. The last thing she needed was for Verona to come out and ask why Elissa was crumpled in a heap on the floor.

Oh, no reason. Pete just kissed me senseless and evidently boneless, too.

Elissa ran her fingers over her lips. It took a remarkable amount of restraint to not follow Pete into his room. She took a deep breath and let it out slowly. Either this was going to be the best relationship of her life or it was going to end very, very badly.

THE NEXT MORNING, Elissa's nerves hummed as she left her room and entered the kitchen to find Pete already there leaning against the counter and drinking a cup of coffee. Really, how had she never noticed how good he looked in that uniform?

"Pulled the morning shift, huh?"

"Yeah, and I don't seem to mind this morning." He grabbed her around her waist and pulled her close for a kiss. He tasted like coffee, banana bread and intoxicating maleness.

The part of her brain that didn't want Verona to know about them screamed for her to pull away, but that warning got shouted down by the rest of her brain and her entire body. How could she say no to something that felt this good?

Pete moved his lips to her ear. "She's already gone."

A shiver ran down her spine at the rumble of his voice, which suddenly sounded husky and sexy next to her ear. As if she wasn't about to combust enough, he gave her earlobe a playful bite. If she didn't get out of here soon, they were going to end up naked. And despite the fact that she was traveling down a different road with Pete, she wasn't quite ready for naked to happen.

Elissa took a step away from him, but in the next moment she lifted her hand to his black eye. "This really is a doozy. Does it hurt?"

"I'd be lying if I said no."

"Guess it comes with the career choice, huh?" And though she'd never really thought about it before, Elissa knew in that moment the fear in Pete's mother's heart even though she'd never stood in his way of doing what he really wanted to. A memory of Pete's dad's funeral flashed through her mind, and with it the visceral need to somehow keep Pete safe.

"What's wrong?"

She met his eyes. "Nothing. I just need to get going. I'm meeting with the contractor today."

"What time?"

"Ten? Why?"

He shrugged. "Just curious." But then he pulled her to him and gave her another one of those bone-melting kisses.

This time, she was the one to pull away. She wanted to tease him the way he had done to her the night before, but the concern utmost in her mind came out instead.

"Are we treading dangerous water here?"

Pete cupped her face and ran his thumb over her cheek. "Probably. But I don't feel like I have a choice."

She didn't, either.

"I'm willing to chance it if you are," he said. "Because either I act on this attraction or go crazy thinking about it."

Her entire body sprang to hot, buzzing life at the intensity of his words and the way he was looking at her.

Pete shifted his thumb to run it over her bottom lip. "We'll go slow." He nodded toward the door to the garage. "Now you better go."

She saw a hunger in his eyes that said that if she didn't leave, that going-slow thing might get tossed out the window and she'd be late for her appointment with Brett.

While part of her liked that idea, she instead used her common sense and headed for the garage.

But during her entire drive to work, she couldn't stop imagining where their kisses might end up. Even as she began shifting everything that was salvageable out of the area of the building that was damaged most severely, her imagination went wild. It conjured scenes of Pete slowly removing her clothes, lifting her in his arms and carrying her to bed, making her cry out his name so loudly that all of Blue Falls heard her.

She couldn't believe how quickly she'd gone from thinking of Pete as merely a friend to a potential sex partner. And this wasn't just one of those friends-with-benefits situations, either. What she was feeling toward him had nothing to do with friendship and everything to do with finding out if the other half of his body was as sexy naked as the top half.

By the time Brett arrived for their meeting, she felt as if she needed to go take a leap in the lake to cool off. She certainly hoped that Brett wasn't a mind reader.

The two of them were standing outside the front of the building talking about the time schedule for the repairs when Pete showed up.

"Hey," she said. "What are you doing here?"

Before answering her, he extended his hand to Brett. "I see you won the bid."

"Thankfully."

Pete turned his attention to Elissa. "Can I talk to you for a minute?"

Wondering what in the world could be so important that he'd interrupt her meeting, she excused herself from Brett and followed Pete to the edge of the graveled area that had been covered with large planters, trellises and birdbaths.

"Is something wrong?"

"No. I just wanted to tell you that I thought of a way for you to save some of the money toward your expansion."

"You found a money tree in my backyard?"

"No, though that would be nice." He glanced past her to where Brett stood. "Just hire him to do the big, structural rebuild, anything where you have to pass codes. I can help you do the inside work, painting, drywall, that kind of stuff."

His offer touched her, and she wondered if she felt it so deeply because her feelings for him had changed. "You don't have to do that. You already have a full-time job."

"Which doesn't require me to work twenty-four hours a day." Pete took one of her hands between both of his and smiled. "Don't argue."

Her independent streak tried to rear its head, but she shoved it down. What he was offering would help alleviate some of her financial stress, and they could spend time together without anyone being suspicious.

"Thank you." She wanted to kiss him, but she wasn't ready to declare their tentative new state publicly. If it didn't work out, she didn't think she could stand everyone looking at her with that knowledge in their eyes, with pity or accusation depending on whom they blamed for the breakup.

She shook her head, telling herself she had to stop thinking negatively. She never really did about anyone else she went out with, but then none of them had been a friend with whom she'd shared confidences, a friend who had trusted her with his own hopes and dreams.

Elissa compromised and hugged Pete. "Thank you." She quickly pulled away and headed back to discuss the new plan of action with Brett. When she reached him, she glanced back at Pete just in time to see him smile at her, a smile that made her skin tingle.

If she didn't mess this up, she was so going to bed with that man someday.

OVER THE NEXT few days, Pete nearly drove Elissa crazy. Now that she'd given him the green light to explore where their new relationship might go, he found every opportunity he could to steal a kiss, everything from a quick peck to ones so hot and thorough that she'd swear her mind was going to melt.

Toward the end of the week, they rode down to San Antonio together to pick up a bunch of stock on the cheap from a nursery that was closing up shop after the death of its owner.

"I can't believe they had this stuff cheaper than I could order it wholesale," she said as they finished loading the last of the planters.

"Guess they just want to be done with it. I can understand."

Elissa experienced a pang at the memory of how Pete had sold his mother's house to the first person to express an interest. He hadn't wanted to drag out the process of dealing with her estate. He'd never said so, but Elissa knew him well enough to realize that he'd been about at the breaking point after months of watching his mom slip away.

Once they were in the truck and Pete had pulled out from the Blooming Rose, he glanced over at her. "You hungry?"

"Is Texas hot in July?"

After hitting the nearest drive-through, Pete drove them to a small park next to a man-made lake. A family of ducks floated along the surface of the water as Elissa and Pete walked to a picnic table at the water's edge.

"I didn't even know this park was here," she said as she sat on top of the table with her feet on one of the concrete benches.

"We used to stop here on our way home from my grandmother's before she died," he said. "I haven't been here in a long time, though." He stared at the water for several seconds, seemingly lost in his memories. "You know, sometimes when I wake up in the morning, I forget that everyone is gone. Even though I hadn't lived with Mom in years, I almost expect her to come in and jerk my covers off to wake me up like she did when I was a kid."

Elissa's heart broke for him even though she knew he wasn't seeking sympathy. She reached over and gripped his hand. "I know it's not the same, but Verona and I consider you family. India and Skyler, too. I'm a firm believer in family being what we make it."

Pete looked at her so long that she felt it all the way down to her bones. "I feel the same about you all," he said. "Even before things started changing between us." He lifted her hand to his lips and kissed it.

"It's crazy, isn't it? How one minute we're just buddies, and in the next something shifted out of the blue?"

"I'm trying not to dissect it," he said.

She wondered if he was afraid of what he'd find if he did.

Elissa retrieved her hand, and they ate in silence for a few minutes. When she was down to the last couple of bites of her burger, she stared at it. "Skyler swears that one of these days all this food I eat is going to catch up to me."

"You never stop moving long enough to gain any weight." Pete wadded up his burger wrapper and pitched it into the trash can.

"Too much to do to sit still."

"Seems like you're sitting still to me."

She looked over at him and wondered again how she'd gone for years without really appreciating how handsome he was. "Who says I'm not doing anything? Thinking is doing something."

He smiled a little. "Oh, yeah? What are you thinking about?"

"I'll give you one guess."

"About how awesome I am."

She laughed. "Who knew there was an ego buried under mild-mannered Pete Kayne's exterior?" Elissa slid off the table, tossed away her trash and headed back toward the truck.

Before she realized what he was doing, Pete caught her around the waist and spun her around so that her back was to a live oak tree. When he pressed close, her breath caught and her heartbeat accelerated.

"How about I tell you what I was thinking?"

She shifted and felt the unmistakable bulge in his jeans. "I think I can tell." Her voice sounded raspy and a touch breathless.

Pete lowered his mouth to hers and captured it in a kiss that could only be described as hungry, as if he were a man who hadn't eaten in a very long time and was starving. Elissa's pulse jumped at that thought as she ran her fingers through his hair. She didn't like the idea that he might have appeased his hunger with anyone else.

"This is so crazy," she said against his wet lips.

"Maybe we both need a little crazy right now."

She liked the sound of that so much that she matched his hunger as they kissed some more. It didn't take long for her body to start demanding more. She was on the verge of ripping his shirt off when the sound of a car door closing somehow penetrated her thoughts.

Pete must have heard it, too, because he jerked away from her and glanced around the tree toward the parking lot. He cursed under his breath before looking back at her. His expression softened in a way that caused her heart to swell. No one had ever looked at her like that. Sure, she'd had lots of interest from guys, had a lot of fun playing the field, but this was deeper, something born of genuine affection. In that moment, as insane as it might seem, she thought maybe she'd just fallen a little in love with him. That thought should have scared her, but it didn't.

Pete dropped a quick, sweet kiss on her lips before adjusting his hat, then taking her hand and casually escorting her to his truck, nodding at the young mother and her three kids as they passed them.

"Well, they almost got a show they weren't bargaining for," Pete said.

The comment was so unexpected that Elissa snorted.

Pete laughed at her. "Nice. How did I overlook that sexiness all these years?"

Elissa shoved him away, but her entire body tingled at the thought that Pete might think her sexy. As they got into the truck and Pete turned them toward home, her mind spun with how quickly things were changing between them. She wondered if the attraction had somehow been there all along, building up without her knowledge until it exploded. Because the way she felt now, she imagined this was how people felt who either had been falling for each other for a long time or had fallen in love at first sight. She and Pete were neither; instead, were some sort of hybrid.

When they turned into the nursery's parking area, Brett waved at them from where he was talking to one of the guys working on the front of her building.

"Now, that's what I call a shopping trip," Brett said as he walked toward them when they got out of the truck.

"Well, I thought, 'Hey, I'm not bleeding enough money. Let me go fork over some more.'"

Brett laughed, and she glanced at Pete in time to see his expression tighten. Jealousy wasn't usually an attractive trait, but there was something about seeing it on Pete's face that made her feel funny. Even though she was about as independent as a gal could get and didn't need protecting, there must still be some sort of primitive instinct that liked when a man appeared as if he'd willingly go to war for her.

To his credit, Pete hid it better than a lot of guys would have and he didn't say anything. That told her he trusted her, and that was sexier than anything he could have said.

Brett waited until Pete had lifted a large terra-cotta planter from the back of the truck and started to walk away before he spoke again. "So, you have any plans after you get this unloaded? I hear there's a good pizza place in town." Evidently, he was willing to give going out with her a second chance.

It took some effort, but Elissa didn't allow herself to look toward Pete. "I already have a date, with a shower and about ten hours of uninterrupted sleep."

"Maybe another night, then."

Elissa made a noncommittal sound as she reached into the bed of the truck for a bag of wildflower seeds.

"Need any help?"

"No, we've got it. But thanks."

Brett seemed to take her subtle hints and nodded before heading back toward his crew.

Elissa watched Pete as they unloaded the rest of the supplies. He didn't say one word about Brett, but by the time they finished she was having a hard time not smiling at how set his jaw was and the way he looked toward Brett every couple of minutes, as if he was making sure he wasn't approaching again.

Wanting to put him out of his misery, not to mention feeding her own desire, she caught him in the back room where they were storing everything until the rebuild was complete. He was about to exit the room, but she pushed him back inside and up against the wall. This time she took the initiative and captured his mouth with hers. Fire raced along her veins. Nothing in her life had ever felt so good.

DESIRE FLOODED THROUGH Pete with a ferocity that caused him to imagine stripping Elissa naked right here and taking her against the wall. That was his base animal talking, though, not the man who knew that women liked to be wooed and romanced.

But wasn't Elissa the one who'd attacked him?

She ran her hands up his chest, and he moaned into her mouth in response. Without thinking, his hands went to her hips, pulling her even closer. This time, she made a sound of appreciation that lit him on fire.

Elissa broke the kiss, leaving him breathing hard.

"That's so you don't worry about Brett," she said.

"I didn't say I was."

She smiled that smile of hers that won over everyone she met. "You are not as good at hiding your emotions as you think you are."

At the moment, he wasn't sure if that was a good or bad thing. Because he was pretty sure he was falling in love with her, falling fast and hard.

Elissa stepped back and started walking away as if she hadn't just pinned him to the wall and kissed him half-senseless.

"Where are you going?"

She looked back over her shoulder and offered him a mischievous grin. "You know what they say about paybacks." With a laugh, she left him standing there as hard as the stone garden ornaments he'd lugged in here and wishing he hadn't teased her the other night. Paybacks were indeed hell.

Chapter Twelve

Elissa watched as India adjusted Skyler's veil. They both looked so happy, and they both deserved every moment of happiness that came their way after the sadness they'd both endured growing up in families that were broken in different ways. By comparison, her life had been nothing but puppies and rainbows. For a moment she was afraid that she'd used up all her good fortune, that the happiness she felt now when she was with Pete or even thought of him was fleeting. That her life's allotment of happiness would run out just as she was beginning to think she might find the type of all-consuming joy her friends had.

"You know, it'll be your turn next." India looked at Elissa as if she could read her thoughts.

A glance at Skyler showed that she was still worried about Elissa getting involved with Pete. It was enough to allow doubt to worm its way inside her.

"I don't know."

"How are things with Pete?"

Elissa turned away and adjusted a part of her pale green dress that was perfectly fine the way it was. "Okay."

"Come on. When have you ever been so secretive about a guy?"

Elissa took a deep breath before turning back toward her friends. "Since I care so much about one that it scares me."

India smiled so wide that it would have lit up a dark room. "That's wonderful. Details, woman. We need details."

Elissa looked at Skyler. "Not now. It's Skyler's big day."

"Oh, no. Don't use me as an excuse."

"You surprise me. I figured you wouldn't want to hear anything about it."

Skyler's forehead wrinkled. "Why not?"

"Because you're against it."

"I never said that. You've just been very casual in the past, but there's something different about you now. I've never seen you look so… Like you're giddy or on pins and needles."

"Like she can't wait to see him again," India offered.

Elissa paced across Skyler's bedroom at the ranch house she now shared with Logan. "I feel as if it's all some wild dream that I'm going to wake up from and be really embarrassed about the next time I see Pete."

"It can't be a dream," Skyler said. "Because I better be getting married today."

"It's real, all of it," India said, looking from Skyler to Elissa.

"So, is he a good kisser?" Skyler asked.

"Yes." Elissa's body flushed with heat at the memory of their kiss in the storage room.

Skyler laughed. "Well, that was a quick answer."

India sat on the edge of Skyler's bed. "I always knew Pete was a good-looking guy, that he'd make someone a good husband."

Elissa held up a hand. "Whoa. No one said anything about getting married."

"He's not just another guy," Skyler said.

"I know that. It's just…I don't know how long this can last, even if I want it to." Elissa leaned against the dresser. "If Pete gets into the state police academy, I don't want anything to stand in his way. Not even me." Her heart hurt at the thought of him leaving Blue Falls, where she couldn't see him every day.

"If things are meant to be, they have a way of working out," India said. "Skyler and I are both living proof of that. Neither one of our marriages would have been a good bet when we met Liam and Logan."

"I'm just afraid of getting too attached." She shook her head. "Honestly, I'm afraid I already am."

"Do you love him?" Skyler asked.

"I've always loved Pete. How can anyone not love him?"

"But are you in love with him?"

Elissa let the question bounce around in her head for a few moments before she answered. "I think so."

"Has he said he loves you?" India asked.

Elissa shook her head.

"I'd bet this ranch that both of you are too afraid of saying it first."

Elissa kept thinking about what Skyler had said all the way through the wedding. As she watched how Logan looked at Skyler, as if he wanted to eat her up, Elissa found herself wanting Pete to look at her like that. When she searched the reception gathering for him, her heart thudded extra hard. The look wasn't exactly the same, but the way he was looking at her made her body throb with longing. The man staring at her wasn't the friend she'd known since they were teenagers. This was a man who had one thing on his mind.

Liam walked up to Pete, drawing his attention away.

"If you don't take that man to bed soon, I think he might die of longing."

Elissa looked at India, who had slipped up next to her without her noticing. "If I do that, there's no going back."

"Do you want to go back?"

"No. But what if he leaves? Do I risk getting that involved? I remember how badly you and Skyler were both hurt when Liam and Logan left and you thought you wouldn't ever see them again."

India wrapped her arm around Elissa's waist. "Sometimes you just have to go on faith."

Elissa had always been fine with living each day as it came, grabbing on to snatches of happiness, okay with letting one go in search of another. She'd never really thought about why, but she supposed it was how she'd gotten used to living life before coming to Blue Falls. Something different every day. Not that it was bad, just different. Now that she looked back, she wondered if she'd held on to that aspect of her old life out of habit while somewhere deep inside she'd been craving stability, an anchor, being able to determine her path for herself. She'd thought living with Verona, going to high school in one place was the answer. But what if it was more than that, and it had taken her nearly fifteen years to figure that out?

What if she'd been searching for someone instead of something or someplace? Was Pete that someone? Had a part of her known that all along and she was just too busy living her life to listen?

She was ready to find out.

"I'll see you later." She ignored the little knowing laugh from India as she made her way over to Pete, who was by himself again. "I'm ready to leave."

It took him a moment, but she saw when her meaning registered.

Elissa managed to keep her hands to herself and act no differently toward Pete than she ever had until they reached her SUV. Even then, they didn't speak as she made the drive back to town and parked in the garage. Not wasting any time, she slipped out of the vehicle and went inside the house, Pete right behind her. As soon as he closed the door, she turned toward him.

"I'm not gonna lie. It scares me how much I want you right now."

Pete closed the distance between them. "I would never hurt you."

"Skyler's afraid I'll be the one to hurt you."

"You'd never do that."

"How can you be sure?"

"Because you're worried that you might." He tugged her close and kissed her deeply. "How long do you think we have before Verona gets back?"

"I don't care. That's what locked doors are for." Before she lost her nerve, she took his hand and led him toward her bedroom. She didn't turn on the light as he stepped inside and she closed and locked the door.

Pete stepped up behind her and kissed her neck. The feel of his lips against her skin sent delicious shivers skittering through her body. She pressed her palms against the door as Pete's hands skimmed up her ribs slowly. Her breath caught when he cupped her breasts. Instinctively, she pressed forward against his hands. Evidently sensing her mounting desire, he spun her toward him.

"You can tell me to stop any time you want to."

She looked up at him in the dark and knew there would be no stopping. "If you stop, I might have to hurt you."

He laughed, low and husky, before taking her mouth with a possessive urgency that had her hands going to the front of his shirt, releasing buttons with fingers that felt suddenly clumsy and inept. When she finally freed the last button, she ran her hands up over all that warm, taut skin, relishing the contours.

"If the women of Blue Falls knew what you hid under here, I'd have to beat them off with a two-by-four."

He laughed a little under his breath. "I doubt that."

"Trust me." To punctuate her point, she planted a lingering kiss on his left pectoral.

In the next moment, his hand snaked through her hair and he brought her mouth up to his. He backed her against the door and kissed her as though they were going to outlaw kisses the next day. His lips moved from hers to her cheek, then down to her neck. When he shoved the edge of her V-necked dress and a cup on her bra aside and captured her breast in his mouth, she gasped and threw her head back. She grasped the back of his head and pressed him closer. He licked and nuzzled, but when he pulled her more fully into his mouth and suckled, she thought she might climax before they even took their clothes off.

Though she hated to break the contact, she pushed him back, shoving his shirt off his shoulders and down his arms in one motion. In the next moment, she lifted the bottom of her dress and pulled it off.

Pete made a sound of appreciation that sent flames dancing along her skin. He pulled her close and unclasped her bra, then threw it somewhere on the other side of her room.

"You seem to be very good at that," she said.

Pete brought his mouth to her ear. "I hope you say that about other things before the night is over."

She gripped his biceps as a wave of undiluted desire surged through her. Never had she imagined Pete saying anything so dang sexy, something that was making her vibrate with longing. She slid her hands to his belt and started unfastening it. This time, she was the one to whisper in his ear.

"Then these pants have got to go."

Pete took over the removal of his pants. When they dropped to the floor followed by his underwear, her mouth went dry. She didn't have to have full light to tell that he was finely cut, that he had a body that was made for what they were about to do.

Next he slid his fingers under the top edge of her panties and slowly slid them down her legs. He kissed his way back up her right leg at a painfully glacial pace. When he reached her thigh, she thought she might collapse. But that was nothing compared to where he moved his mouth next. He nudged her legs apart and captured the most intimate part of her with his mouth, licking and sucking and delving into the very core of her. If not for the door at her back and bracing her hands against his shoulders, she would no doubt collapse in a heap on the floor.

Pete's hands took a firm hold on her hips as he increased the pace of his tongue. Elissa banged her head back against the door as she moaned with a pleasure so intense she never wanted it to stop. In the next moment, Pete delved even deeper and she came in a wonderful rush.

As if he knew how close she was to collapsing, Pete stood and swung her up into his arms. He crossed the room and laid her on her bed. She barely had time to take a breath before he'd sheathed his erection and was poised to enter her.

He looked down at her. "You're sure?"

"Positive."

He filled her in one smooth thrust that had her on the verge of another climax. Again, she threw her head back, against her pillow this time. She clawed her sheets as Pete slowly withdrew before sliding in again. Her body took over as she lifted her hips to match his thrusts, each one a little bit faster than the last. Pete's warm hands cupped her hips, helping to set the increasing pace.

"You feel so good," he said.

She searched for a response, but her brain was too scrambled to form words. Instead, she wrapped her legs around his back and captured his mouth with hers. Her actions seemed to light a fire in Pete as he moaned like an animal and let go of any restraint he might have had.

They weren't quiet and there would be no mistaking what was going on if Verona came home, but Elissa flat-out didn't care at the moment. "Faster," she breathed.

Pete complied, and Elissa felt another orgasm building inside her. Each thrust brought her closer and closer and…she tensed as she broke apart inside. A moment later, Pete cried out and found his own release. She continued to move against him, riding this glorious moment for all it was worth. But finally, Pete collapsed against her while still holding up enough of his weight that he didn't crush her and remaining inside her.

She let her legs drop back to the bed and ran her hands up Pete's sweaty back. As spent as she felt, her need was so intense that she immediately wanted him again.

"You've been the master of false advertising," she said.

Pete lifted his head to look down at her. "You weren't satisfied?" He sounded hurt, so she brought her lips to his to give him a kiss that she hoped showed him how she felt better than any words she could cobble together.

When they broke the kiss, she lifted her hand to rest against his face. "Everyone thinks you're the good guy, the epitome of the boy next door."

"I'd like to think I am a good guy."

"You are. But there's some bad boy in there, too."

His mouth stretched into a crooked, pleased-with-himself smile. "So you did enjoy yourself?"

"To say the least." She shook her head. "I should be embarrassed right now, but I'm not."

Pete gently pushed some of her hair away from her face. "So you're okay?"

As she looked up at him, her heart swelled and she couldn't have been more surprised by her answer. "Yeah. But part of me can't believe what I've been missing all these years. And right next door."

"I guess we'll just have to make up for lost time, huh?"

Her eyes widened as he shifted, revealing that he was aroused again. "That was quick."

He kissed her in a way that stoked her own desire. "I guess you just have that effect on me."

When he slid farther inside her, she lifted her hand to the back of his head, running her fingers through his hair and adding an urgency to their kiss. She was so caught up in how wonderful he felt that she didn't understand immediately why he stopped moving. But then she heard Verona's footsteps approaching, and her breath caught. Elissa's heart rate increased as Verona got closer to her door. Only when the footsteps passed by and Verona's bedroom door closed did Elissa let out her held breath. When she met Pete's eyes, they both burst out into hushed laughter.

"I suddenly feel like I'm a teenager again, sneaking around," she said.

Pete lifted an eyebrow. "You hid someone you were having sex with in your bedroom?"

"No, that's not what I meant." She playfully swatted him on the arm. "Just because I've dated a lot doesn't mean I've gone to bed with all of them." She ran her finger along his collarbone. "Very few actually."

"I'm glad to hear that." Pete kissed her forehead, then her cheek, nuzzled her ear. "Do you want me to go?" He moved his hips, caressing the innermost part of her.

"No."

They made love again, slowly and careful to be quiet. As she came again, she wanted so badly to be somewhere she could cry out. Instead, she kept the sound of her pleasure under wraps. There was something oddly erotic about having to be so contained, as if she knew she was building up to some future lovemaking that would rock her world.

When Pete slid to her side and gathered her back against him, she felt as if she could happily stay right where she was for the rest of her life.

WHEN PETE WOKE in the predawn hours, the last thing he wanted to do was leave Elissa's bed. A part of him was afraid that if he did, he'd discover it had all been a dream. And he wanted what they'd done to be real, and to have it happen again. In fact, just thinking about it had him hard and nearly panting to wake Elissa by making love to her.

Instead, he gently pushed her mussed hair away from her face and kissed her cheek.

Elissa rolled toward him, snuggling close. He closed his eyes and relished the feeling of her like this, naked and comfortable in his arms. He couldn't help worrying that she would regret it all under the harsh light of day, that she would try to ignore that it had ever happened as she had their first kiss.

He didn't realize she was awake until she started kissing his neck. When her hand drifted down to encircle him, he went rock hard.

"Don't," he somehow found the willpower to say.

"Why not?"

"Because I need to get back to my room before Verona wakes up."

Her tongue ran over his right nipple. "We still have time."

"You're killing me."

Elissa pushed him onto his back and rolled atop him. "I seriously doubt that."

It was all he could do not to cry out when she took him inside her. When she began to rock her hips, he was a goner. Even if Verona found out, there was no way he could leave Elissa now, not when her body was making his come alive. He ran his hands up her ribs to her breasts.

"You're so beautiful," he said.

He couldn't tell for sure in the dim light, but he thought his words surprised her. How could they? She had to know how beautiful she was. After all, she never lacked for male companionship and she'd once been the Belle of Blue Falls beauty queen.

She leaned down to kiss him, and he felt so much emotion in that kiss that it gave his heart a kick. It was on the tip of his tongue to tell her he loved her, and that shocked him probably as much as it would her. But he kept it inside, not willing to scare her off. Having her in his arms like this was the best moment of his life, and he wasn't going to part with it willingly.

He lifted himself to a sitting position, bringing her with him. She wrapped her legs around his hips, a movement that nearly had him coming apart before he wanted to. Needing to taste more of her, he captured one of her breasts in his mouth. When Elissa threw her head back and rocked against him, he knew he'd never seen anything more beautiful in his life.

Pete gripped her hips as she rode him until he almost couldn't see straight. After he came, she continued to move for a few more seconds until her entire body stiffened with her own release.

Elissa felt as limp as a noodle as he fell back. She lay on his chest, her naked breasts pressed against him. The entire world outside her room could go up in flames and he was afraid he wouldn't care as long as he could hold her like this.

But he wanted to protect her, too, and that meant not letting Verona know what was going on until Elissa was ready. As much as he hated to, he shifted away from her. He half expected her to try to stop him, but this time she didn't. Instead, she openly watched him as he slipped out of bed and got dressed.

"You looked nice all dressed up last night," she said. "And you're sexy as hell when you're wearing your typical cowboy clothes. You even do nice things for that uniform of yours. But I have to say you look best wearing nothing at all."

He smiled. "So are you saying I should walk around Blue Falls naked?"

"Only if you want to cause wrecks and give little old ladies strokes."

He laughed before bending down to give her a long, deep kiss that he hoped had her thinking about him all day. How he was going to get through his morning shift, he had no idea.

"Talk to you later, okay?" he said.

She nodded and then gave him another quick peck before he headed for the door.

He listened for a moment before opening the door as quietly as he could. Mentally crossing his fingers that Verona wasn't awake, he eased open the door to the guest room and stepped inside.

Even though he'd had more sex in the past eight hours than he had in, well, a very long time, he already wanted Elissa again. He had no idea how he could suddenly crave someone who'd been his friend half of his life, but there was no denying it. And he was already counting down the hours until he could be with her again.

He only hoped that she felt the same way, that he didn't go the way of so many other guys she'd dated. He was going to do everything in his power to ensure that Elissa didn't feel the need to seek male company elsewhere. And that meant, oddly enough, getting out of this house and into his own place, somewhere neither one of them would have to hold back the next time they fell into bed with each other. So as soon as he finished his shift, he was going to see Skyler and convince her that he needed that apartment now.

Chapter Thirteen

Elissa lost count of how many times she had to refocus her attention on work. Her thoughts kept going back to the night she'd spent with Pete, how it almost seemed like the hottest, most erotic dream she'd ever had. She still couldn't believe how Pete had begun things with her, how many times they'd made love, how very, very good he was at all of it. Her friend had been hiding a sex god underneath that uniform and cowboy hat. And she had the overwhelming desire to keep that knowledge to herself, to make sure she was the only one who ever saw that side of him.

Despite all the work she had to do pricing the new stock, updating her computer system and periodically checking on the construction progress at the front of the building, the day seemed to drag by. She'd fantasized about dozens of ways they could be together again without Verona knowing. She just wasn't ready to face her aunt's "I told you so," especially since she had no idea what the future held for them. For right now, she just wanted to focus on the moment and worry about the future later.

"Hey, looks like the new construction is coming along pretty well."

Elissa looked up from her desk to see India standing in the doorway. "Yeah. Brett added a couple of guys to the crew to get it done faster."

India sauntered into the room and sat on the edge of the desk. "Probably thinks that'll help his chances of going out with you again."

Elissa shrugged. "Can't help what people assume."

"You really should tell him you're off the market."

"Why do you say that?" Elissa was afraid she already knew the answer.

India pointed at Elissa and made a circular motion toward her head. "Because you have that I-had-sex-last-night face."

Elissa sat back and let her head drop against the back of the chair. She cursed under her breath. If India could tell, then the moment Verona saw Elissa she was going to be making wedding plans.

"I knew it!"

Elissa looked toward the door. "Keep it down, would ya?"

"I can't help it. I'm just so excited."

"Why?"

"Well, gee, I can't imagine. Oh, maybe it's because two of my best friends have found out they're perfect for each other."

"You never said anything about me and Pete before."

"I didn't know either of you was interested in the other."

"We weren't." She hesitated a moment. "How is that even possible, being friends one moment and then wanting to jump his bones the next?"

India's smile widened. "Good, huh?"

Elissa thought about how she'd told herself she wanted

to keep what she and Pete had shared secret, but she couldn't stand it a moment longer. She had to talk to someone. "Unbelievable. I've barely been able to think about anything else all day."

India shook her head. "You are seriously messing with my worldview. Sweet Pete Kayne is a hottie in bed."

"In bed, out of bed, he's just a hottie, period."

"So, what now?"

Elissa leaned forward onto the top of her desk. "I don't know. To be honest, I'm afraid of looking too far ahead. This could just be a fling that's burning hot and will flame out soon."

"You don't really think that." India sounded so certain that Elissa met her friend's gaze.

"I'm afraid of saying it out loud, afraid of jinxing it, but no. This feels...different somehow."

"Like you're all jittery inside, like you're dying of thirst and Pete is the only water in the world?"

"Yeah."

India placed her hand atop Elissa's. "Hon, you're falling in love."

"But I'm not the falling-in-love type. Everyone knows that."

"Maybe you were never serious with anyone because it wasn't the right person."

"But Pete's always been there. Why now?"

India shrugged. "Right timing? One of the great mysteries of the universe? Who knows? But don't analyze it to death. If it feels right, it probably is."

"But how do I know for sure? I don't want to hurt him."

"Don't give what Skyler said another thought. Besides, she can see the difference in you, too. The old

Elissa would be taking advantage of that good-looking man working on your building. But no, you're in here daydreaming about someone else. When was the last time you did that?"

Never.

"Exactly," India said, as if she'd heard the word in Elissa's head. "Take my advice, and don't overthink it."

That was easier said than done, proven by the fact that Elissa was completely useless after India left. She alternated thinking about making love to Pete again and worrying that if things fizzled between them there was no way to salvage their friendship. Not after what they'd done the night before. She wasn't even sure that she wouldn't die of embarrassment the moment she saw him face-to-face again.

As the sun began to set, she heard footsteps coming toward her office. Her heart rate increased until she realized the sound was work boots and not cowboy boots like the ones Pete wore. In the next moment, Brett appeared in her doorway.

"We're packing it in for the night."

"Okay, thanks for all the work today. It's already looking a lot better."

"We aim to please." With a smile, he walked away.

Elissa stared at the empty doorway. It was the first time Brett hadn't tried to flirt with her, and she wondered if he could tell the same thing that India had. Wow, when had she become so transparent?

With the work crew leaving for the day, she was free to go home, as well. She shut down her computer and made sure the building was secure before walking out into the parking lot. She stopped in her tracks when she spotted Pete standing next to her SUV with a bouquet of flowers in his hand.

Feeling giddier than she ever had over a high school crush, she smiled and crossed the distance between them. "I didn't expect to see you out here."

"Were you expecting someone else?"

"Oh, you caught me. My supersecret boyfriend was supposed to pick me up for a hot night on the town."

Pete pulled her close. "Is that right? Well, I just might have to arrest this boyfriend and introduce him to one of our county's finest jail cells."

"I thought you all had a full house."

"As luck would have it, we happen to have a couple of vacancies."

"Well, I can't be seen dating a jailbird, now, can I?"

"How do you feel about a lawman?"

"Depends."

"On?"

"On how soon he stops talking and kisses me."

Pete's smile melted her heart just before his mouth captured hers in a kiss hot enough to rival the Texas heat. What India had said about being thirsty and Pete being the only water ran through Elissa's head, and that's exactly how she felt with Pete's arms around her and his mouth doing things to hers that made her brain go on the fritz.

Eventually, Pete stepped back and offered her the flowers.

"How am I supposed to explain these to Verona?"

When her eyes met Pete's, there was something there looking back at her, some emotion she couldn't quite name, before it disappeared in the next moment.

"Maybe you could keep them somewhere else."

"I guess I could put them in my office."

"I have another idea." He took her hand in his and led her toward his truck.

"Where are we going?"

"It's a surprise."

Willing to go along for the ride, she slid into the passenger seat. When he made the turn into the parking lot for the Wildflower Inn, she thought maybe they were going to dinner there. But as he led her toward the building, he didn't head for the front door. Rather, he took the path that led to the exterior door to Skyler's old apartment.

"What's going on?"

He didn't answer. Instead, he slipped a key into the lock and opened the door for her. She gave him a curious look before she stepped inside. Just when she thought Pete couldn't surprise her any more, he did exactly that.

The dining room table had two covered dishes, lit candles and an empty vase the perfect size for her multicolored bouquet. Soft music played in the background.

"Skyler lent you her apartment?"

"No, it's my apartment now."

That surprised her so much that she spun toward him. "You moved out?"

He stepped close to her and caressed her cheek. "I took a leap of faith that I might be needing more privacy."

"Oh." An uncharacteristic flush of heat flowed up her neck to her face.

"Was I wrong?"

Her thoughts went back to the previous night and how she'd been unable to stop replaying their lovemaking in her mind all day. "No, you weren't."

He kissed her softly before taking her hand and leading her toward the table. "We better eat before it gets cold."

But food wasn't exactly what Elissa was hungry for at the moment. She stopped walking and tugged back on Pete's hand. At his questioning look, she said, "That's what microwaves are for."

Desire flickered in his eyes. "Then I guess I'm lucky that Skyler left her old one here." He ran his fingertips up her bare arm, sending delicious shivers along her skin. "What did you have in mind?"

Instead of telling him, she started walking backward, towing him toward the bedroom. When they stood next to the bed, she wasted no time ridding him of his clothing, tossing his Stetson halfway across the room. He got caught up in her urgency and helped her out of hers. When they fell back on the bed, she was more than ready for him as he drove his way home.

They'd taken their time and kept as quiet as possible the night before, but tonight was different. Their lovemaking was fast and frenzied, and she felt her climax building within moments of them beginning. A rush of excitement went through her. Slow, thorough lovemaking was a wonderful thing, but this, this had its merits, as well.

Pete cupped her hips and increased his pace. His breath was hot and heavy near her ear. "Don't hold back."

And she didn't. She let herself go, meeting his thrusts and moaning in pleasure. When she found her completion, she cried out his name, asking him to keep her pleasure going as long as possible. So he did, until he finally climaxed, too.

Pete collapsed beside her. "I really think you've killed me this time."

"Not a bad way to go, huh?"

He laughed and kissed her. Lying with him like this, naked and spent, was the most wonderful feeling in the world. She just wished she could kick the feeling that it wasn't going to last.

"What's wrong?"

"Nothing."

"You're lying." Pete rubbed a finger over her forehead. "You get creases here when you're concerned about something."

"I'd rather not say." Because the last thing she ever wanted to be was a clingy female. That wasn't her, no matter how much the desire to hang on to Pete with all her strength might say otherwise.

He skimmed her lips with his fingertip. "We're fine, Lis."

She hoped he was right.

After a lovely dinner and another round of lovemaking, Pete held her hand as he led her out to his truck. But instead of taking her back to her vehicle, he drove in the opposite direction.

"Where are we going?"

"To see a friend."

That friend ended up being Frankie. "Hey, boy," Pete said as they entered the barn. "Did you miss me?"

Elissa would swear from the look in Frankie's eyes that he understood Pete and would have said yes if he could talk. She stepped up next to Pete and rubbed her hand along Frankie's smooth neck.

"Want to go for a ride?" Pete asked.

"I think I already did that."

Pete laughed. "Naughty girl."

She smiled up at him. "I try."

He dropped a quick kiss on her lips before saddling Frankie and leading him from his stall. Frankie nearly pranced with excitement. Pete scratched the horse between the ears. "I haven't had time to ride as much since the tornado. Ol' boy's feeling neglected."

"Well, we can't have that." Elissa let Frankie sniff her hand.

Pete helped her onto Frankie's back, then swung up behind her before guiding Frankie out of the barn and toward the trail that ran around the edge of Glory's property.

It was a clear night, and out here away from the lights of town the sky stretched out like a star-studded black canvas. Elissa had visited some of the most awe-inspiring places in the world, but she couldn't imagine being anywhere else at the moment. This slice of Texas was home, but what was beginning to feel more like home was the man behind her. She closed her eyes and breathed in the night air, listened to the clop of Frankie's hooves against the ground, relished the feel of Pete's arms and legs around her.

"You're awfully quiet," he said near her ear.

"Just enjoying myself."

"Me, too." He kissed her lightly next to her ear and fell back into silence.

They didn't say much on the ride, just enjoyed the peace and quiet, simply being in each other's company. After Pete guided Frankie back to the barn, Elissa wandered outside to wait for Pete. Happiness welled up inside her so much that it scared her a little. She pushed the concern aside as Pete came out of the barn and took her hand as they walked toward his truck. The only time he let go was when he had to walk around to get in the driver's side.

When they returned to the nursery, Pete parked beside her SUV.

"I won't push you," he said. "But some time soon, I want you to spend the night with me. I don't want you to worry about if someone knows."

She leaned across the truck and kissed him so that she wouldn't have to say anything. A part of her wanted to proclaim their relationship to the world, but there was still enough fear in her heart that things wouldn't work out that she just couldn't, not yet. Not when doing so would mean a constant barrage of questions and expectations from Verona. She loved her aunt dearly and knew that she meant well, but she could be intense with the need to pair everyone up.

Even so, it was remarkably difficult to drive away from Pete. When she pulled into her garage, she didn't immediately get out of the SUV. Her emotions felt as if they were spinning like the contents of a blender. Excitement over her new relationship with Pete, sadness that he wasn't going to be right next door anymore, anxiety about allowing herself to think too far into the future. After all, how likely was it that she was going to hit the true-love lottery after both India and Skyler had? Wasn't that asking too much from fate?

Realizing that the longer she sat in the garage, the more likely Verona was to question her, she got out and went into the house.

"Hey, hon," Verona said. "How's Pete?"

Elissa stopped moving just as Verona looked up from her knitting.

"Oh, don't look so surprised," Verona said. "You're

not nearly as good at hiding things from me as you think you are."

"What do you mean?" If Verona said one word about knowing that Elissa and Pete had been having sex when she came home from the wedding, Elissa was going to die of embarrassment.

"That you're head over heels in love with that boy."

Elissa didn't even try to argue. There was no use. Instead, she crossed to the couch and sank down onto its edge. "It's totally insane, right?"

"Why would you say that?"

"It's Pete," she said, as if that should explain everything.

"Yes, and you couldn't find a better man if you tried the rest of your life."

"But we've been friends with no hint of attraction for years."

"Are you sure about that?"

Elissa looked at her aunt. "What does that mean?"

Verona smiled. "When you moved in, Pete had the biggest crush on you."

"No, he didn't."

"Just because he never said anything doesn't make it any less true."

That revelation floored Elissa. "Do you think he's felt that way all this time?"

"That's something you'd have to ask him."

Elissa flopped against the back of the couch. "Why wouldn't he say anything?"

"Maybe he was afraid to, or maybe it went away and only recently reignited. What about you?"

Elissa shook her head. "I never thought of Pete that

way. I mean, I knew he was attractive, but he was just my friend."

"But something changed."

"Yeah. I think it's the out-of-the-blue nature of it that scares me. What if it goes away just as suddenly?"

"Does it feel like that's going to happen?"

Elissa thought about that for a moment, then shook her head again. "No."

Verona smiled, the way she did when she'd known something all along.

"Don't tell me you knew this was going to happen."

"Why do you think I tried to nudge you two toward each other? I saw the glances and the subtle changes in how you acted around each other even before either of you realized what was happening."

Elissa stared at her aunt for several seconds. "You are a freak of nature."

Verona laughed, and in the next moment Elissa found herself laughing, too.

"So, when do I get to start planning your wedding?"

Elissa threw up her hands and stood. "This is why I didn't want you to know."

Verona laughed again and gave Elissa a look that let her know she was teasing.

Elissa shook her head. "A freak of nature and evil, I tell you. You've got everyone snookered into thinking you're this sweet little lady, but I know the truth." She grabbed and playfully tossed a ball of yarn at her aunt, then headed toward her bedroom.

"Mark my words, wedding bells will ring for you two."

Elissa closed her bedroom door behind her, blocking some of the sounds of giggling from the other room. But once she took one look at her bed and remembered what she'd shared with Pete there the night before, she couldn't help imagining what it might be like if Verona's prediction came true. It was so hard to believe. For now she was happy to revel in the high of being with Pete in a way she'd never dreamed of before that tornado had blown him into her guest room.

She walked to the bed and stretched out along its length. As she closed her eyes, she inhaled Pete's scent and smiled.

Chapter Fourteen

Over the next week, Elissa discovered she was happier
each day than the day before. She'd always considered
herself a happy person, but she'd had no idea how happy
she could be until now. When they weren't working, she
and Pete spent almost all of their time together. They
went for a canoe ride on the lake, to a movie in Austin, to a dinner on the River Walk in San Antonio and
for another horseback ride, this one on the trails at the
Teagues' ranch. They also spent plenty of time at Pete's
apartment in his bed.

Even now, as she watched the construction guys put
the finishing touches on the rebuild, she couldn't stop
thinking about him and when she'd see him next.

"Would you like to take a look at everything?" Brett
asked as he approached.

She shifted her attention back to what she should be
concentrating on, getting her business back up and running so she stopped falling deeper into a financial hole.
"Sure."

As she followed him through the tour of the new construction, excitement built in her. Maybe two or three
days of interior work and she could open again. "You've
done a great job. And I really appreciate the fast tracking."

"My pleasure."

"Come on and I'll get the last of your payment."

Brett followed her to her office as his employees loaded up their equipment. He leaned in her doorway as she wrote him a check. When she extended it to him, she found him watching her with a look she knew well.

"So you and the cop are an item now?"

Something about the phrasing "an item" didn't sit well with her. They were much more than that, though she was still hesitant to put a definitive name to it. "We're dating, yes."

He shook his head. "All the good ones are taken." He took the check. "Well, if you're ever free, you have my number."

"I do." But she hoped she never had the need to call it again, at least not for the reason he was implying.

With a little salute, he turned and walked away. After a few moments, she stood and left her office to lock the exterior door. But when she reached it, she noticed Pete passing Brett on his way toward her. When Pete reached the door, she smiled but didn't open the door.

"I'm sorry, sir, we're closed."

He tapped the badge pinned to his uniform shirt. "It's in your best interest to open the door, ma'am."

"Is that right? I can't imagine why I'd want to do that."

He stepped closer. "Open the door and I'll show you."

Giggling, she slipped the lock free. The moment he stepped inside, Pete pulled her to him and kissed her as if he hadn't seen her in a month.

"I take it you missed me," she said.

"How did you figure that out?"

She pointed toward her temple. "My finely honed powers of deduction."

Pete rubbed his palm down her arm. It was the simplest of touches, not anywhere near as erotic as so much else they'd shared, but something about it lit her on fire. An idea formed in her mind that had her reaching around him and securing the door.

"Can you help me move something in the back?"

"Sure."

Elissa led the way to a large room filled with patio furniture, some of which had just been delivered that morning in anticipation of her reopening. They were halfway across the room when she spun around and pushed him down onto a chaise longue. She followed him and started unbuckling his belt.

"What are you doing?" he asked.

She gave him a wicked grin. "I'd think that was obvious. I have to say, Deputy Kayne, you do fine things for a uniform." She leaned forward and whispered in his ear, "Especially when I know what is beneath it."

Elissa captured his mouth as she wriggled out of her shorts and underwear and freed him. She didn't take the time to remove his boots or even his pants all the way before she settled herself onto him.

They made love fast and with a lot of heavy breathing before they both found their release and she collapsed atop him.

"You are insatiable," he said as he smoothed her hair.

"I know. It's like you turned some sort of switch on inside me."

He tilted her face to look up at him. "Is it really that different with me?"

She caressed his cheek. "Yes. I'm afraid of jinxing it by saying it, but I've never felt this way before. I feel like I've been saving up all these years and I can't get enough of you."

He smiled. "Who am I to argue with that?"

She almost told him that she loved him, but still something kept her from saying those words that she knew in her heart were true. She loved Pete Kayne with all her heart.

He hadn't said the words, either, but she found herself hoping that he held the feelings. Everything pointed that way, including when she arrived at work the next morning to find not only Pete and her employees on hand to help with the painting and interior organization but also almost a dozen other people, too. India and Liam, Skyler and Logan, Lara, who worked in India's store, a couple of the inn's employees, Greg Bozeman, Keri and Simon, and a few other Teagues quickly got to work as she indicated what needed to be done.

Halfway through the morning, she looked up from painting the trim around the entryway into the new section of the building to find Pete smiling at her. "What?"

"You have paint on your nose."

"And you find that funny?"

"Cute."

As he came close, as though he was going to kiss her, she lifted her brush and dabbed it against his nose, leaving a white smudge of paint behind.

She saw the change in his expression that promised retribution and turned to flee. But he was too quick. He caught her around the waist and spun her into a little alcove full of decorative outdoor thermometers. Before she could say anything, he kissed her so deeply that her head spun.

Someone knocked loudly on the wall, causing them to

jerk apart. "Come on, lovebirds," Simon said. "Don't be leaving the rest of us to do the work while you make out."

Elissa hid her face against Pete's chest. He dropped a kiss onto the top of her head before leading her out of the alcove.

A few minutes later, Skyler stepped up next to Elissa. "I'm so happy for you."

"Yeah, it'll be great to get the doors open for business again."

"That's not what I meant."

Elissa looked over to see Skyler watching Pete. "I'm happy for me, too."

With the amount of help Pete had brought, all the necessary work was completed by the end of the day. If she allowed a day for the paint to fully dry and to get the word out that she was reopening, she could be back in business in two days. After everyone but Pete left, she found him in the patio furniture room with a naughty grin on his face.

"Care for an encore?" he asked.

"How about we both go home and take showers, put on clean clothes and actually go out for a meal?"

"I suppose that's doable. As long as you promise I can have you for dessert."

She laughed as he pulled her down onto his lap and kissed her.

"Thank you, for everything you did today."

He shrugged. "I have to keep up my good-guy appearance, especially when you're endangering my reputation."

"Me?" She jumped to her feet and stepped out of his reach. "I might have to reconsider that dessert." As she backed away, he just smiled at her.

"You won't be able to resist me."

The thing was she knew he was right. And she wore a stupid smile all the way home. She couldn't even wipe it from her mouth as she stepped inside. Why did it matter? Verona had been at the nursery today, a witness to their not-so-secret kissing in the alcove. Plus, Verona already had a good idea how besotted Elissa was with Pete anyway. Heck, the entire Hill Country probably knew by now, and she no longer had a problem with that.

When she stepped inside, she heard the shower running. While she waited for her turn in the bathroom, she grabbed the stack of mail on the kitchen counter and started going through it. Bills, junk mail, a postcard from her parents. She flipped it over and read her mother's writing.

Just a quick note to let you know we're off to a couple of weeks in Chile. Then we're coming for a visit. Looking forward to seeing you, dear.
Love,
Mom

She smiled at the thought of seeing her parents. It had been three months since she'd last seen them. They likely had a million and one fascinating tales to share, and she certainly had a few things to tell them, too. She set the postcard aside and went through the rest of the mail. Her smile faded when she reached the last envelope. She bit her lip as the full impact of what she held in her hand hit her.

It was addressed to Pete, from the Texas Department of Public Safety. She didn't have to see the contents to know what it said. They had accepted him into the academy, and he would leave.

Tears pooled in her eyes as her heart broke.

PETE HELD ELISSA's hand in his as he led her into his apartment. That simple contact between them felt so right. He still couldn't believe how their relationship had changed seemingly in the blink of an eye. But he was glad it had. And it was much more than sex. He knew without a doubt that he loved her. Now he just had to find the right time and place to tell her, something that she'd remember for the rest of her life.

But first he had to find out what was bothering her. Though she'd tried to hide it, her mind had been elsewhere all through dinner. Whatever it was, it had to have happened between the time they left the nursery and when he'd picked her up to go to Gino's.

Pete tugged her into his arms. "What's wrong?"

"Nothing."

He cocked his head slightly to the side. "I'm a cop, remember? I know when someone isn't being truthful."

She sighed as she stepped away from him and walked to the dining room table. She set her purse down on the table and dug inside it until she pulled out an envelope.

"Here," she said as she extended the envelope to him. "This came for you today."

As soon as he took it and saw the return address, his heart rate increased. And the way Elissa was reacting to the letter told him something else, that she cared enough about him that she didn't want him to leave.

"This won't change anything," he said.

She gave him a sad smile. "It will, Pete. And it should. You've wanted this the entire time I've known you."

He lifted his hand to her face and ran his thumb across her cheek. "It's not the only thing I want. I love you, Lis." It wasn't how he'd wanted to tell her, but he could already see her pulling away. He didn't think he could handle that.

"You've had to put your dream on hold too many times," she said. "You're finally free to pursue it, and I'm not going to be the reason you don't."

He held up the letter. "You don't even know what it says."

"I do, Pete. Because there's not a person in Texas better suited to be a Ranger. You're the ultimate good guy."

With a shake of his head, he ripped the envelope open, halfway hoping it was a rejection. But it wasn't. He'd always imagined how happy he'd be in this moment, but he'd never imagined it might mean losing the woman he loved. Well, he wasn't willing to do that.

"I don't have to go," he said.

"Don't do that," Elissa said, sounding angry. "If you throw away this opportunity, I'll never forgive you."

He stared at her for several seconds and knew she wouldn't change her mind. "Fine, I'll go. But that doesn't mean anything between us has to change."

"The academy is what, twenty weeks? And then you could be stationed anywhere in Texas."

"That doesn't mean I'm going to the back of beyond."

"It doesn't mean you aren't, either. Listen, let's not make this harder than it has to be."

"What's that supposed to mean?"

Sadness filled Elissa's eyes as she stepped close enough to caress his face. "You've been there for me every step of the way as I've worked toward my dream. Now I'm trying to return the favor."

He saw what she meant to do, and it hit him hard in the chest. "Lis, don't do this."

"Isn't it better that we step away before we get in any deeper?"

"No, it's not. You know why? Because I couldn't fall for you any more than I already have."

He saw the struggle reflected in her eyes, but for some reason she wouldn't allow herself to say the words that he had to believe were in her heart. He'd never seen her be with anyone else the way she had with him.

Elissa rested her hand against his heart. "You mean a great deal to me, Pete. That's why I want you to do this, to go where it leads you."

"How am I supposed to go away and leave you behind?"

"You've had this dream of following in your father's footsteps long before you even knew me."

He started to protest, but she placed her fingers against his lips.

"Do this for me, Pete. Go to the academy, become a trooper. After everything you've been through, you deserve this. And if you stayed here, you might wake up ten years down the road and resent the fact that you passed up this opportunity."

"A job isn't everything."

"No, but we both know that this is more than a job to you. It's a calling."

He knew Elissa well enough to realize that he could argue until he was blue in the face, and she wasn't going to budge. He'd just have to find another way to show her how much she meant to him, that he was determined to find a way to make it work between them.

But what if she was right? If he made it through the academy and became a trooper, what would happen if he got stationed at the back end of Texas? He couldn't ask her to give up her life here in Blue Falls any more than she seemed to be willing to ask him to abandon his long-held goal of becoming a trooper and eventually a Texas Ranger.

He bit down on the need to curse. She must have seen his turmoil because she stepped closer and kissed him. It felt like a goodbye kiss, and that made something shatter inside him. He had a pretty good idea that it was his heart.

IT WAS A SHORT drive between the inn and Elissa's house, but she had to pull over on the side of the road halfway there. She sobbed like a baby. She'd always considered herself a strong person, but it had taken an entirely new level of strength to walk away from Pete. The fact that he'd professed his love for her had nearly shaken her resolve to let him go. But she'd seen marriages fall apart because one person had given up too much for the other. Skyler's parents were a prime example. It always led to resentment or worse. She couldn't bear the thought of those types of harsh feelings existing between her and Pete.

Because she loved him, too, more than she'd ever loved anyone. She'd commiserated with both India and Skyler when they thought they'd lost the men they loved, but until this moment she'd had no idea how intense that kind of pain could be.

A part of her hoped that fate would smile on them, that he would complete the academy and be posted nearby so they could pick up where they left off. But she couldn't bank on that. By the time he completed the academy, he might not feel the same way anymore. She swiped at a fresh swell of tears that came on the heels of that thought.

After a few minutes, she managed to pull herself under control. Not willing to answer a bunch of Verona's questions, she grabbed several tissues from the box in her console and wet them with some bottled water. She wiped the tear tracks from her cheeks and dabbed at what had to be her red, swollen eyes.

By the time she pulled away from the side of the road, half an hour had passed. She wanted nothing more than to curl up in her bed and be left alone to replay all the wonderful memories she had of her time with Pete. Or maybe it would be a better idea to try to push those memories away.

Any hope of escaping to the privacy of her room, however, disappeared when she reached her house and noticed her parents' car in the driveway. She took a few moments to plaster on a facade that wouldn't announce her true feelings and headed inside.

"Hey, sweetie!" Elissa's mom hopped up from the couch and rushed toward her, then wrapped her in her arms. "It's so good to see you."

"You, too, Mom. You should have called and we could have had something special planned."

Her mom waved away the very idea. "Seeing my baby girl is special enough. Plus, I wouldn't want to intrude on your social life. Verona says you're dating Pete Kayne. I always thought he was a cutie."

Elissa shrugged. "We've been out a couple of times, nothing serious." She didn't dare meet Verona's gaze, and she hoped her aunt stayed quiet.

"And here I was hoping I might have some grandchildren to spoil some time before I'm too ancient to remember their names."

Elissa forced a laugh. "I'd say we have a while before that." She sensed Verona approaching, so Elissa guided her mom back to the couch. "So, I want to hear all about your recent adventures."

Over the next hour, they talked about all her parents' latest travels, the tornado and the grand reopening of the nursery in a couple of days. Eventually, her mom started yawning.

"So sorry," she said. "I guess the jet lag is catching up to me." She reached forward toward her empty glass on the coffee table.

"I'll get that, Mom. You and Dad go on to bed."

As everyone stood, Elissa's dad pulled her into his arms and kissed the top of her head the way he had when she was a little girl. "I'm glad you're safe, punkin. When I heard about how close that tornado came to you, I nearly had a coronary."

Elissa hugged her dad tightly, partly because she was glad to see him but also because she needed some comfort after breaking things off with Pete.

As her parents started down the hallway, Elissa grabbed the dirty dishes from the coffee table and headed to the kitchen to put them in the dishwasher. She realized her mistake of not making a beeline for her own bedroom when she turned to find Verona standing at the entrance to the kitchen.

"What's going on with you and Pete?"

"Nothing. We had a little fun, and now it's over. You know I'm not the settling-down-with-one-guy type."

"Bull."

Elissa startled at the intensity of Verona's response.

"You may have been that way before, but Pete changed you."

"You're mistaken."

"It's about the letter from DPS, isn't it? He's going to the academy."

Elissa's bottom lip quivered. She bit down on the involuntary reaction, but she wasn't quick enough to keep Verona from seeing it. Her aunt came closer.

"You're pretending you don't love him so he'll go, aren't you?"

There was no hiding anything from her aunt, so why try? "You know him. He won't go if he thinks he has a reason to stay."

"Shouldn't that be his decision?"

"You don't know how much this means to him, how much it's always meant. He shouldn't have to give up his dream because of me."

"Oh, hon. I think you underestimate Pete."

"How so? He's done it before. He's the type of guy who always puts himself last. It's not fair."

"What's not fair is you lying to him."

"I didn't."

"But you're not telling him the entire truth, either."

Elissa let out a long sigh. "It's my decision, and it's done." Unable to talk about Pete anymore without falling apart again, she walked past her aunt and retreated to her bedroom. Almost as soon as she closed the door behind her, the tears started falling again. She curled up in her bed. Even though her linens had been washed since she'd shared the bed with Pete, she'd swear she could still smell his scent.

She closed her eyes, but that didn't keep the tears at bay. Not wanting anyone to hear her distress, she buried her face in her pillow and let the sorrow flow.

Chapter Fifteen

"You're doing what?" India and Skyler said in unison.

Elissa glanced around at the customers filling the nursery. While she was happy that the grand reopening was such a success, her heart still weighed heavy. She missed Pete more than she would have ever thought possible. And that was just after a day apart. What would it be like after a week, a month?

"Mom and Dad asked me to go to New Zealand with them, and I'm going. Quite honestly, I need a vacation."

"But you just reopened the nursery," India said.

"And I have competent employees to run it."

India took Elissa's hands in hers. "Are you sure you did the right thing with Pete? I saw him at the bakery yesterday, and he looked like someone had sucked all the light out of his life."

Elissa retrieved her hands. "Don't try to make me feel any worse than I already do."

"But if you both feel this awful, doesn't that tell you something?" Skyler asked.

"I know it's hard now, but if he lets one more thing keep him from following this dream he's had since he was a little boy, I fear he'll never follow it. And he'll live to regret it."

Elissa looked from India to Skyler and back. "And what is that saying, if you love something, set it free? If it comes back to you, it was meant to be. If it doesn't, it was never yours."

Her friends didn't look convinced, but all thoughts of trying to make them see she was doing the right thing faded when she spotted Pete looking at her from across the room. She wanted so badly to run to him, to kiss him and confess that she loved him, too. She didn't know where she got the strength to hold her ground. Maybe someday she'd feel good about giving him the freedom he needed to go after what he wanted, but right now it just carved her up inside.

"I hope you know what you're doing," Skyler said.

Elissa gave her friend a sad smile. "I guess you were right, after all. I did end up hurting him."

Skyler didn't get a chance to respond before India noticed Pete approaching and pulled her away.

"Looks like a good turnout," Pete said as he scanned the crowd.

"Yes, I'm pleasantly surprised."

"I don't know why. You have a great business, and everyone has been waiting for you to reopen so they could support you."

An awkward silence descended between them, and she hated it with every fiber of her being. She desperately wanted back the easy camaraderie, the laughter, the way he made her body vibrate when he kissed her.

"Lis, I've been thinking about what you said, and I haven't changed my mind. I don't want to give up on us."

"Pete—"

"Even if I go, it won't be for another week. I want to spend that week with you."

She swallowed past the lump in her throat. "I won't be here. I'm leaving tonight for New Zealand with my parents."

Pete's forehead scrunched in confusion. "What?"

"I haven't had a vacation in forever, and I've missed my parents. I've always wanted to go to New Zealand, so this seemed like the perfect opportunity."

"Were you even going to tell me?"

"No." She hated being so blunt, but she could see the path his thoughts had been thinking. If he was going to make it in the academy, he had to have all his attention on that, not on her.

"I see." He took a step back, and it felt as if he took a chunk of her heart with him. "I hope you have a nice time."

Pete spun and walked away so quickly that Elissa nearly cried out. Instead, she pressed her lips together and watched the man she loved walk out of the building, wondering if it would be the last time she ever saw him.

ELISSA STARED OUT across the incredible beauty of New Zealand's Lake Manapouri. With the backdrop of the snow-covered Cathedral Mountains, it was truly awe-inspiring. Her eyes knew it; so did her mind. It was her heart that wasn't getting the message. No, it was firmly entrenched a world away.

She wiped away a tear as her parents approached.

"Breathtaking, isn't it?" her mother said as she came to stand next to Elissa.

"It is." And she suddenly wished Pete were here beside her, to see this wonder with her.

Elissa glanced at her father as he made his way on

down the trail, pausing to take photos from different vantage points.

"We can get you to the airport by early evening."

Elissa jerked her attention back to her mother. "What?"

"Sweetie, it's obvious you're not really here."

"I'm sorry. I guess I'm just tired. It's been an exhausting few weeks."

"I might not be around all that often, but I am your mother. I know when you're fibbing, and I know when you're hurting. And right now you're doing both."

Elissa shook her head. "It doesn't matter. What's done is done."

"The only thing that is irreversible is death. Now, we're going to take you to the airport, where there's a ticket back to the States waiting. I know you're stubborn, but you forget you get that from me. Within five minutes of seeing you that first night back, I knew you had changed. You thought you hid it, but I could see you'd been crying. After I'd talked to Verona, it all became clear."

"But I can't stand in his way."

"Darling girl," her mother said as she smoothed a few loose hairs out of Elissa's face. "Pete is a grown man, entitled to make his own decisions. And by all accounts he's head over heels in love with my daughter. After everything he's been through, all he's lost, don't you think he deserves to be with the woman he loves? The woman who loves him?"

Elissa felt like a fool because she hadn't thought of it that way. She'd thought she was doing the right thing.

"What if I'm too late?"

"Somehow I doubt that boy has fallen out of love with you that quickly."

The burning need to get back to Pete rushed through Elissa. She had to tell him how she felt and hope that she hadn't ruined everything.

"What time is my flight?"

Elissa's mom looked past her. "Come on, Henry. Our girl's got a plane to catch."

THE TRIP HOME from New Zealand felt like an eternity, as if she were coasting to the edge of the universe. When she landed in Austin, she wanted nothing more than to rush straight to Pete. But she had no idea where he was staying since the academy didn't have housing. Plus, after darn near twenty-four hours of airports and cramped planes, she probably looked as worn as she felt.

So she drove home, planning exactly what she would say to Pete. She tried not to think about what she'd do if he told her she was too late, that she'd hurt him too much for him to forgive her.

When she drove down her street, she noticed India's vehicle parked in her driveway. As soon as Elissa stepped into the house, India wrapped her in a hug.

"I knew you'd come to your senses." India pulled back and grabbed Elissa's hand. "Now come on. We've got work to do."

Verona shook her head. "I told them you'd need to get some sleep before you go see Pete."

"No, I just came home to grab a shower and some clean clothes. I'm wearing three continents."

"Told you," India said. "I know this crazy, can't-wait-another-minute feeling." She looked back at Elissa. "Go shower. We'll be waiting for you in your bedroom."

Her nerves sparking at the idea of being able to see Pete soon, she took her time showering, using her sweet pea shower gel, washing her hair and shaving her legs. She didn't want to look or smell like something that had just been dumped out of the cargo hold of a plane when she saw him again. The idea was to win him back, not make his nose turn up.

When she reached her bedroom, she found her two best friends at the ready with makeup, hair products and a new dress, shoes and jewelry from India's store.

"You didn't have to do this," Elissa said as India and Skyler went to work on her.

"Are you kidding?" Skyler said. "And miss the chance to say, 'We told you so'?"

Elissa rolled her eyes, but she didn't fire back. Her friends could say whatever they wanted as long as Pete still loved her.

PETE WALKED OUT of the academy building alongside Carl and Shondra, two of his fellow trainees.

"I feel like I could eat an elephant," Carl said. "You all up for barbecue tonight? I hear Spivey's is good."

"Sounds good," Shondra said.

"Pete, you in?"

He thought about declining, but sitting in his motel room alone again didn't hold a lot of appeal, especially when he imagined Elissa on the other side of the world playing tourist and not giving him a second thought. He kept going back and forth between believing she'd been telling the truth when she said she just wanted him to follow his dream and thinking it was only an excuse to get out of a relationship that had gone too far for her.

"Sure, sounds good. I'll meet you guys there in half an hour."

"Make it an hour," Shondra said. "I think we all need showers after today."

"Maybe you do. I barely broke a sweat," Carl said.

"Yeah, you just keep thinking that, Stinky."

Pete laughed at them as he headed toward his truck. He drove the few miles to his motel, pulled into the lot and parked on autopilot. It wasn't until he stepped out and started walking toward his room that he saw something that shocked him so much he froze. He blinked a few times, not trusting his eyes.

"Hello, Pete." Elissa, she was real, standing beside his door wearing a blue-and-white dress, threatening to rob him of his very last breath.

"What are you doing here? I thought you were in New Zealand."

"I was until yesterday. Or the day before." She shook her head. "I don't even know what day it is. I've spent most of the last twenty-four hours trying to get here."

His heart picked up its pace despite the fact that he was trying not to get his hopes up. "Why?"

"Because I'm a fool."

"Didn't like New Zealand, huh?"

She smiled at him, and he'd never seen anything so beautiful.

"I loved it, actually." She took a step toward him. "But not as much as I love you."

"Lis—"

"No, let me finish. I've been practicing this across I don't know how many time zones. What I did had nothing to do with my feelings for you, unless you count how much I want you to have everything you've ever wanted. You are the nicest, most decent man I've ever met, and you've had more bad things happen to you than anyone deserves. I knew how much you wanted to become a trooper and then a Ranger, so when you said you loved me I was afraid you would allow that to keep you from following your dream. But I realize how wrong I was in not telling you the whole truth, that I'm totally crazy in love with you, too. I understand that I may have ruined everything, and—"

He closed the space between them. "Will you stop talking and let me kiss you?"

She looked stunned, as if she really thought that he could have stopped loving her so quickly. Unable to resist her any longer, he pulled her next to his body and kissed her deeply with all the love he felt for this woman.

"Does that mean I'm forgiven?" she asked.

"You've taken a good first step."

"Do I want to know what the other steps are?"

He dropped a soft kiss on her lips. "Don't worry. I think you'll enjoy them."

She smiled up at him, making him the happiest man on the planet.

"This doesn't change the fact that I don't know where I'll be stationed."

"It doesn't matter."

"I can't ask you to give up your dream any more than you could ask me to give up mine."

She reached up and cupped the side of his face. "Dreams change, and you're my new dream. Besides, I can operate a nursery anywhere. Who knows, maybe I'll open a second location for Paradise Garden."

"Well, in that case…" He pulled his phone out of his pocket and dialed Carl's number.

"You're making a call?"

"Yes, very important business."

"Yep?" Carl answered.

"Hey, man, I'm going to have to take a pass on dinner. Looks like I'm going to be busy."

"What could be better than barbecue?"

"How about the woman I'm madly in love with?"

"Oh, yeah, I can see where that's better than barbecue."

Pete ended the call and slid his key card through the door's lock. And then he scooped Elissa up into his arms and carried her inside, kicking the door closed in their wake. She yelped, then laughed, and he had the deep need to make her laugh for the next sixty or so years.

He set her on her feet at the end of the bed. "You know, I almost flew to New Zealand to find you."

"Why, after the way I treated you?"

"I had something I thought might change your mind." He turned and opened a drawer behind him, retrieved a small box from below his T-shirts. "I thought it might be romantic to propose to you someplace a little more exotic than Blue Falls."

Elissa gasped when he popped open the box to reveal an engagement ring that he'd spent the entire day after she'd left picking out, calling himself nine kinds of fool all the while.

"Oh, Pete."

"I know a motel room is even less romantic than Blue Falls, but I'm not willing to wait a minute longer in case you disappear again." He lowered himself to one knee. "Elissa Jane Mason, will you marry me?"

"Yes." She dropped to the edge of the bed and claimed his mouth with hers. "And I promise you I'll never disappear again."

He slid the ring onto her finger, his heart beating

wildly and his mouth stretching into a smile that felt as if it were consuming his entire body.

Elissa looked down at the sparkling diamond on her finger, then back at him. "I just have one request."

"What's that?" Right now she could request anything and he'd move heaven and earth to get it for her.

She trailed the hand with the ring over the top of the bedspread. "It would be an awful waste to have this bed and not use it, don't you think?"

He ran his hands up her bare legs. "It would indeed." He stood and brought her with him down onto the bed. He caressed the edge of her face. "I love you, Lis, and I'll spend the rest of my life trying to make you happy."

She smiled up at him. "You don't have to try. You make me happy just being you."

Unable to find the words to tell her how happy she made him, he gave her a kiss filled with all the love he felt for her.

"I know this sounds crazy, but I'm glad that tornado blew my house away."

She looked horrified. "Don't say that. You could have been killed."

"But I wasn't, and if it hadn't happened I might never have known that the perfect woman for me was right next door."

"Well, if you put it that way." Elissa began unbuttoning his shirt. "I guess we have a lot of lost time to make up for."

"I think you're right." He captured her lips again and set about making up for that lost time.

* * * * *

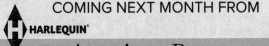

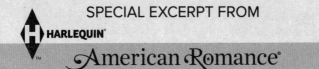
A long-held secret finally comes to light for this rugged
cowboy. Can Will go from a part-time cowboy living in a
bunkhouse with his brothers to a family man?
Find out next month in
HER SECRET COWBOY by Marin Thomas

Will Cash pulled off the road and parked next to the mailbox at the entrance to the family farm. As usual the box was stuffed. He gathered the envelopes and hopped into the truck, then directed the air vents toward his face. Normal highs for June were in the low nineties, but today's temperature hovered near one hundred, promising a long hot summer for southwest Arizona.

He sifted through the pile. Grocery store ads, business flyers, electric bill. His fingers froze on a letter addressed to Willie Nelson Cash. He didn't recognize the feminine script and there was no return address. Before he could examine the envelope further, his cell phone rang.

"Hold your horses, Porter. I'll be there in a minute." Wednesday night was poker night, and his brothers and brother-in-law were waiting for him in the bunkhouse. If not for the weekly card game, they'd hardly see each other.

He tossed the mail aside and drove on. After parking in the yard, he walked over to the bunkhouse, opening the letter addressed to him. When he removed the note inside, a photo fell out and landed on his boot. He snatched it off the ground and stared at the image.

What the heck?

Dear Will… He read a few more lines, but the words blurred and a loud buzzing filled his ears. The kid in the picture was named Ryan and he was fourteen years old.

Slowly Will's eyes focused and he studied the photo. The young man had the same brownish-blond hair as Will did, but his eyes weren't brown—they were blue like his mother's.

"Buck!" he shouted. "Get your butt out here right now!"

When Buck came out, the rest of the Cash brothers and their brother-in-law, Gavin, followed.

"What's wrong?" Johnny's blue eyes darkened with concern.

Will ignored his eldest brother and waved the letter at Buck. "You knew all along."

Buck stepped forward. "Knew what?"

"Remember Marsha Bugler?"

"Sure. Why?"

"She said you'd vouch for her that she's telling the truth."

His brother's eye twitched—a sure sign of guilt. "The truth about what?"

"That after I got her pregnant, she kept the baby."

The color drained from Buck's face.

The tenuous hold Will had on his temper broke. "You've kept in touch with Marsha since high school. How the hell could you not tell me that I had a son!"

Look for HER SECRET COWBOY,
the next exciting title in The Cash Brothers *miniseries,*
next month from Marin Thomas

HARLEQUIN®

A *Romance* FOR EVERY MOOD™

Stay up-to-date on all your
romance-reading news with the
Harlequin Shopping Guide,
featuring bestselling authors, exciting new
miniseries, books to watch and more!

The newest issue will be delivered right to you
with our compliments! There are 4 each year.

Signing up is easy.

EMAIL

ShoppingGuide@Harlequin.ca

WRITE TO US

HARLEQUIN BOOKS
Attention: Customer Service Department
P.O. Box 9057, Buffalo, NY 14269-9057

OR PHONE

1-800-873-8635 in the United States
1-888-343-9777 in Canada

Please allow 4-6 weeks for delivery of the first issue by mail.